"You're A Tough Man To Bargain With."

For a split second his expression altered, allowing her to catch a glimpse of the business predator he rarely revealed to her. Jack was a man who played for keeps and she'd do well to remember that.

Then another thought struck. What if he had another purpose for reconciling with her tonight? What if it had been only because he still needed her…versus he cared about their relationship more than his vendetta against the Kincaids or his desire to clear his name?

Jack paused in the process of clearing their plates from the table. "What's wrong?" he asked. "You look upset."

Nikki shook her head, avoiding his gaze. "It's nothing."

She was wrong. She had to be. Jack wouldn't use her like that.

Would he?

Dear Reader,

What a fun project this has been! I can't begin to tell you how much I've enjoyed writing the ministories that have appeared at the end of each of the books leading to this one. It allowed me to give you a peek into the evolving relationship between Jack and Nikki, something I've never had the opportunity to write before. If you haven't read the other books, I urge you to pick them up. Not only are they fabulous stories, but you have the extra treat of reading about the building love affair that leads to the start of *A Very Private Merger*.

As many of you know from the books I write, I love creating large families and then exploring each of their stories. This series fits right in. Not only does it explore the dynamics of the Kincaid family, it also allowed me to write a book about a man who's spent his life on the outside, longing to be part of a family he's been excluded from since birth. How many of us have reached out, hoping against hope that someone will take our hand? How many of us have been too afraid to make the attempt? Watch as Jack decides whether to risk it all… with the help of a very special woman.

Welcome to *A Very Private Merger*, a story of redemption, of learning to trust and of creating that special bond with family. Oh, yes… And of course I couldn't resist adding my usual touch of humor. Enjoy!

Warmly,

Day Leclaire

DAY LECLAIRE

A VERY PRIVATE MERGER

™ **Harlequin**®

Desire

Special thanks and acknowledgment to Day Leclaire
for her contribution to the
Dynasties: The Kincaids miniseries.

Recycling programs
for this product may
not exist in your area.

ISBN-13: 978-0-373-73175-6

A VERY PRIVATE MERGER

Copyright © 2012 by Harlequin Books S.A.

www.Harlequin.com

Printed in U.S.A.

DAY LECLAIRE

USA TODAY bestselling author Day Leclaire is described by Harlequin Books as "one of our most popular writers ever!" Day's tremendous worldwide popularity has made her a member of Harlequin's "Five Star Club," with sales of well over five million books. She is a three-time winner of both a Colorado Award of Excellence and a Golden Quill Award. She's won *RT Book Reviews* Career Achievement and Love and Laughter Awards, a Holt Medallion and a Booksellers' Best Award. She has also received an impressive ten nominations for the prestigious Romance Writers of America RITA® Award.

Day's romances touch the heart and make you care about her characters as much as she does. In Day's own words, "I adore writing romances, and can't think of a better way to spend each day." For more information, visit Day at her website, www.dayleclaire.com.

To my readers who have followed me through the years.
My thanks. My gratitude. And my love.

* * *

Don't miss a single book in this series!

Dynasties: The Kincaids
New money. New passions. Old secrets.

Sex, Lies and the Southern Belle by Kathie DeNosky
What Happens in Charleston... by Rachel Bailey
Behind Boardroom Doors by Jennifer Lewis
On the Verge of I Do by Heidi Betts
One Dance with the Sheikh by Tessa Radley
A Very Private Merger by Day Leclaire

One

Son of a bitch!

Jack Sinclair stood on the sidewalk outside The Kincaid Group building and watched Nikki Thomas, his soon-to-be-former lover, give Elizabeth Kincaid a hug before heading into the Kincaid complex. As far as he was concerned, it was the ultimate betrayal.

Puzzle pieces he didn't even realize he was missing dropped into place in that instant. She worked for TKG, there was no other explanation. All this time—three amazing months together, an affair unlike any he'd experienced before, one that teetered on the brink of becoming something solid and permanent—and she'd been using him. Setting him up. Working for the enemy. He took a deep breath and reached for the cool, calm poise he'd spent a lifetime cultivating. He found it… but just barely.

There could be some other explanation for that hug,

his few remaining shreds of rational thought insisted. Since Nikki had purchased him at the Read and Write bachelor auction, an affair held at Lily Kincaid's home and attended by half of Charleston's elite, she could have met Elizabeth there. Or through a woman's club they had in common. Maybe Elizabeth and Nikki's mother were friends. They were all part of Charleston high society. No doubt they'd met at some event or another.

It could be just that simple.

Not only that, but Jack had asked Nikki in her role as corporate investigator to find out who owned stock in The Kincaid Group, specifically who owned the key ten percent not controlled by him or the Kincaids. Perhaps she was here on a fact-finding trip. All perfectly innocuous.

Well, there was an easy way to find out. He pulled out his cell phone and touched the screen to access TKG's main phone number. The receptionist answered on the second ring. "The Kincaid Group. How may I direct your call?"

"Connect me with Nikki Thomas, please."

The woman hesitated. "Nikki? Nikki Thomas?"

"She's your corporate investigator. She said I could reach her through this number."

"Oh. Certainly. One moment, please."

He disconnected the call and swore long and hard, his momentary hope for an innocuous explanation sweeping away like the wish for summer in the face of a frigid Arctic nor'easter. He'd known from the start that she was a corporate investigator, but her claim of confidentiality had kept him from asking key questions. Now she'd answer every last one of them.

He headed for the TKG building, driven by something so deep and primal and basic he couldn't put a name to it. He just knew it led to Nikki. To a confrontation with the woman who'd pushed through doors of intimacy he'd spent years barring and locking.

The woman who'd soon regret ever screwing him over.

Jack didn't waste any further time. He crossed the street, oblivious to the busy traffic. His entire focus remained on the four-story building in front of him and the woman who worked there. He'd been inside TKG several times over the past five months for meetings with his father's sons and daughters—the "Legitimates," as he referred to them. No doubt they referred to him as the "Bastard," a nickname he'd earned on more than one front.

He approached the reception desk. The woman seated behind the wide sweep of finely crafted wood took one look at him and snatched up the phone. He reached over the counter and disconnected the call without the least compunction. No doubt she had standing orders to alert one of the Kincaids whenever he appeared. He'd have done the same in their place.

"You know who I am?" he asked, his voice deadly soft.

She nodded mutely.

"Excellent. Then you also know I own a sizable portion of this company." He gestured for her to return the receiver to the cradle. "Nikki Thomas. Where?"

She'd picked up on his anger and intense concern flickered across her face. "What's your business with Ms. Thomas?"

"That's none of your concern. Where is her office? I won't ask again. Nor will I forget your lack of cooperation."

The receptionist's concern grew, along with an almost protective expression. Leave it to Nikki to instill such loyalty in her fellow employees. For a moment, Jack didn't think she'd answer. Then she caved. "Second floor…210," the woman murmured unhappily.

"You will not alert her to my presence, is that quite clear?"

"Yes, sir."

Jack circled the reception desk, debating briefly on whether to take the elevator or stairs. Stairs. Less risk of running into a Kincaid. Considering his current mood he didn't trust himself not to knock the unlucky person flat on their ass. It didn't take long to find Nikki's office. Her door was ajar and though she stood at a large window overlooking the harbor, he doubted she took in the stunning view, not with her head bent and what appeared to be the weight of the world resting on her fine-boned shoulders. In all the four months he'd known her, he'd never seen her look so defeated.

She wore her hair up, exposing the vulnerable paleness of her neck. Brilliant golden sunlight streamed in the window, losing itself in the ebony darkness of her hair while highlighting her potent feminine figure, showcased in a form-fitting royal blue suit. He'd watched her don that outfit just this morning, knew intimately what scraps of silk and lace hid beneath, their color a perfect match to her suit. He also knew—intimately—what she looked like in the panties and bra, how that shade of blue turned her magnolia-white skin luminescent, and how tempted he'd been to strip them away before returning her to their bed.

He clamped down on the surge of desire with a ruthlessness his competitors had come to fear…and respect. She'd betrayed him, something he doubted he could ever forgive. Now he'd find out just how deep that betrayal ran. And he'd know why. He closed the door. The metallic click sounded like the cocking of a trigger, the sound of the lock being thrown as explosive as a gun blast.

Nikki's head jerked up and she spun around, her expression confirming his worst suspicions. He must have still entertained a lingering hope that she'd offer a reasonable explanation for her presence at The Kincaid Group. Otherwise, he'd never have experienced such an overwhelming and devastating sense of loss.

"Jack." His name escaped on a sigh of guilt and dismay.

"I believe there's something you neglected to tell me, Nikki. Vital information that's four months overdue." He didn't dare approach. Not until he'd regained full control of his temper. "Care to rectify that omission?"

"I can explain."

He couldn't help it. He laughed. "How often has a woman said that to a man? Of course, there's usually another man in her bed at the time she uses that expression."

"It's probably as many times as a man's said it to a woman when she comes home unexpectedly to find him making love to someone else," Nikki retorted. Then her flash of anger faded, sliding into something that hovered between sorrow and regret. "I'm sorry, Jack. Saying I can explain is a rather ridiculous comment given the circumstances."

He leaned back against the door and folded his arms across his chest. "I wondered why you were willing to pay so much for me at the Read and Write bachelor auction. You claimed you bid for me because no one else would. But now I suspect it was all a setup. The

Kincaids came up with the clever scheme so you'd be in a position to spy on me, didn't they? It all makes sense now."

She held up a hand and her eyes flashed a swift warning. "Hold it right there. If you think for one minute that I bid on you at the Kincaids' request—"

"You bid a thousand dollars when no one else would." The anger he worked so hard to control escaped his iron grip for a split second. "You set me up right from the start."

She shook her head, the vehement motion causing silky strands of her hair to escape and caress her arching cheekbones, as well as the long sweep of her neck. God, he remembered burying his face in that sweet-scented hair only hours before. Remembered kissing a pathway along the pale, velvety line of her neck. How long would it take before the memories faded and he'd know peace again?

"I didn't set you up. Not then and not now."

She took a single step in his direction, but something in his expression drove her back, a stumbling retreat that brought out the predator in him. She must have sensed it because her breath quickened and her eyes—those damnable sapphire-blue eyes—darkened with pain and regret. She wrapped her arms around her narrow waist which only drew his attention to the fullness of her breasts straining against her suit jacket.

He forced his gaze away, forced himself to focus on her elegant, duplicitous features. They were beyond lovely, no doubt inherited from her mother, the aristocratic side of her family tree. He should have known that someone who'd been born and bred within Charleston's social elite couldn't be trusted. Hadn't his mother discovered that when Reginald Kincaid had made her his mistress?

Angela Sinclair had come from the wrong side of the tracks, which made her eligible for a bed partner, but she'd never been good enough to marry, any more than the son they'd borne together had been good enough to claim. Jack's mouth twisted. At least, he hadn't been claimed until dear ol' Dad had been dead and gone, leaving others to clean up the shattered mess the man had left behind.

All his life, Jack had stood on the outside of those fancy manors, while the Southern gentility had stuck rigidly to their social rules and order. Society had made him an outcast because of his bastard status, while welcoming the man who'd set the double standard, the man who'd proudly embraced the Legitimates, the children he'd fathered with Elizabeth Kincaid. All the while he'd kept Angela and his firstborn son a deep, dark secret. Now for the final piece of irony.

The one woman he'd grown to trust, to respect, whom he believed he could love for the rest of his life and had planned to offer the ring currently tucked away in his dresser drawer, was working for the Kincaids. No doubt their entire relationship had been built on a bed of lies. And hadn't he just enjoyed the hell out of that bed…until now.

Nikki held out a hand. "Please, Jack. You have to believe me. When I attended that bachelor auction and bid on you, I had no idea who you were. I didn't understand why no one else would make an offer. I mean, it was for charity. It didn't make sense."

"You really expect me to believe the Kincaids didn't put you up to it?" He shook his head. "Sorry, sweetheart. Considering you work for them and have kept very quiet about that fact makes it impossible for me to believe anything you have to say."

"I didn't find out until after that first kiss we shared at the auction," she insisted doggedly. "Lily found us by the carriage house, remember? You left and she told me who you were."

Oh, he remembered that first kiss, remembered every second of the overpowering desire that had swept them both away, a desire that made them blind and deaf to everything going on around them. He'd never experienced anything like it before. He rarely lost control, prided himself on keeping his emotions and reactions reined in at all times, safely walled away. But that night... That night he'd lost it, had been ripped in two by an imperative to possess, to mark the woman in his arms in some fundamental, primal way. To make her his in every sense of the word.

Is that what his parents had felt for each other, why they'd flouted society's rules and strictures? He shied away from the thought, unwilling to explore the possibility that allowed any gray into his black-and-white world. Of course, he hadn't made love to Nikki that night. But he had the next time they'd met, when she'd collected on the dinner she'd won at the auction.

Jack stared at her, watching, analyzing, weighing. "Even if I believed you... The Kincaids were all there when you bid on me. They knew you'd won a date with me. Are you trying to tell me now they didn't use that information? You're their corporate investigator, aren't you?"

"Yes, I'm their corporate investigator. Yes, Matt and RJ Kincaid knew about our dinner date. And yes, Matt asked me—"

Before she could finish her statement, the handle of

her office door jiggled. Discovering it locked, whoever had come—no doubt rushing to Nikki's aid—began pounding on the door. Jack frowned in annoyance. Apparently, he needed to work a bit harder on his intimidation skills since clearly the receptionist had called for reinforcements. Although to be fair, he'd only warned her not to alert Nikki of his arrival. He hadn't thought to include the rest of the Kincaids in his demand. The pounding reverberated against the wood, echoing straight through the hollowness filling his chest.

"Your rescue party, I believe." He tilted his head to one side. "Must have been the receptionist. Apparently, her concern for you outweighed my threats."

Nikki's mouth dropped open and a hint of outrage glistened in her eyes. "You threatened Dee?"

"Of course I threatened Dee. It's who I am, remember? I threaten. I act. And then I win."

She shook her head. "That's not true, Jack. That's not the man I've spent the last three months falling—"

Another burst of pounding interrupted her words, words he'd have given half his fortune to have heard her utter. "Sinclair, we know you're in there." His half brother, RJ's voice, Jack decided. Uncannily similar to his own, which only served to add to his anger. Irrational, but true. "Unlock this door right now or we're calling the police."

Jack lifted an eyebrow. "Well? Should I let them in?"

Nikki sighed. "That's probably best if you don't want to be arrested."

"Arrested for what? I own forty-five percent of TKG."

"Jack, please."

He shrugged and did as she requested. Might as well get this over with. He stepped aside, grateful he'd done so when the door banged open. RJ and Matt Kincaid piled into the office. While Matt aligned himself in front of Nikki, RJ confronted Jack.

"Are you all right, Nikki?" RJ asked, his sharp gaze fixed on Jack.

The resemblance between them went beyond the superficial. Both topped six feet by an inch or two and were more solidly built than Matt's lean, swimmer's body. They'd also inherited a substantial portion of their father's aristocratic good looks, including his dark brown hair and the general shape and expression of the eyes, even though the shade of blue differed dramatically. And as loath as Jack was to admit it, they also shared an uncanny knack for business, both excelling at it—which would make Jack's success when he gained control of The Kincaid Group all the sweeter.

Matt, on the other hand, had darker hair and his eyes were the image of his mother's, a sharp, currently infuriated bottle-green. Jack also sensed a strong protective instinct flowing through the younger of the two brothers, possibly due to his son's recent close call with a serious health issue. No doubt that combination of factors explained his current stance in front of Nikki.

"Nikki?" RJ prompted. "You're okay?"

"I'm fine. Jack and I were having a…discussion." She stepped out from behind Matt's broad shoulders. "Perhaps you can help."

"Sure. Get out, Sinclair."

Jack simply laughed. "That's not going to happen."

"Nor is it what I meant," Nikki interceded. "Maybe you could help by telling Jack what you asked me to do in regard to our investigation of him."

Beside her, Matt stiffened. "Are you kidding?"

"I'm dead serious," Nikki replied, her gaze pleading. "Matt, tell Jack at what point you asked me to investigate him and his business. Please," she added in a strained undertone.

Matt hesitated, but Jack could tell from his expression it wasn't in order to come up with a convenient lie, but because he was attempting to pinpoint the exact time frame. "You were on the phone with him, setting up your auction date," he finally said. "After you hung up, I asked you to see if you could uncover Sinclair's plans regarding TKG. Since he now owns forty-five-percent interest in the company we were hoping he'd indicate how he intended to use his shares."

"And," Nikki prompted. She smiled at his concerned expression. "It's okay, Matt. Just tell him."

He shot a resentful glare in Jack's direction. "I asked you to get a feel for the man. Is he someone you would want in charge of TKG?"

"So, you had Nikki investigate me and Carolina Shipping," Jack stated flatly. His gaze turned to Nikki and lingered there for a long, painful moment. Tears filled her eyes and he forced himself not to move, not to acknowledge the impact of them in any way. "I'll expect a copy of any and all reports you've generated about me on my desk by the end of today."

"You can't—" RJ began.

"I can," Jack retorted, cutting him without hesitation. "I'm majority shareholder of this company. I'm well within my rights to request that information. And if it's not on my desk by five, my lawyer will seek a court order forcing you to turn it over to me. Then we'll see just when and what you ordered Nikki to do."

Matt stepped in, frustration ripe in his voice. "You're our competitor, Sinclair. What the hell did you expect us to do? Sit idly by while you dismantle our livelihood?

There's no way you won't attempt to take over our family's business with that forty-five percent you keep waving in our face, just as there's no way you won't attempt to fold TKG into Carolina Shipping." He rested a supportive hand on Nikki's shoulder. It took every remaining ounce of Jack's self-control not to knock it off. The wave of sheer possessiveness that ripped through him felt as overpowering as a tidal wave. "FYI, I told Nikki that if I was wrong and you were on the up-and-up, fine. But you're not on the up-and-up, are you, Sinclair?"

"I am when it comes to business."

"Bull," RJ interjected. "You've been undercutting us from the start, using the murder rap the police attempted to pin on my mother to steal new business away from us."

"True." Jack shrugged. "So what? Business is business."

RJ's mouth tightened and his expression—one eerily similar to what Jack saw in the mirror each morning—sparked with impotent fury. "I won't allow you to take the business our father built and drop it in the crapper."

"Why would I do that?" Jack asked mildly. Oh, he was enjoying taking on the brothers who'd been put ahead of him his entire life. He'd hungered for this moment, just as he hungered for the moment when he'd step into his father's shoes as President and CEO of The Kincaid Goup. "TKG is a highly successful business, one I own considerable stock in. I have no interest in destroying it."

RJ hesitated, his gaze shifting to his brother where the two had a moment of silent communication. "Then what are your intentions regarding the annual meeting later this month?"

"I plan to attend."

Yeah, he was definitely getting too much of a kick out of this. Or he would if Nikki's eyes weren't fastened on him, pleading for his understanding. Oh, he understood, all right. He understood that he should never have trusted someone who moved in the rarified ranks of Charleston's elite.

"We'll be electing a new president and CEO. Who do you plan to vote for?" RJ pressed.

"I could tell you to wait and see, but there's no point." He took a single step in RJ's direction, not the least surprised when his half brother held his ground. He had a strong suspicion they were a lot alike in that regard, too—maybe too much alike—cut in the same mold as the father they both shared. "I plan to take over TKG."

Matt swore. "I knew it."

Jack simply smiled. "And I plan to do exactly what you thought I'd do. I plan to fold TKG into my own company." His gaze blistered first RJ, then Matt. "Welcome to Carolina Shipping. I suggest you don't get too comfortable. You won't be staying long."

And with that he turned on his heel and left the office. He didn't look back, though everything within him urged him to do just that. But he didn't dare. Because he knew that one look at Nikki's devastated expression would gut him.

At precisely five minutes to five Nikki Thomas pulled into Carolina Shipping's parking lot. Jack's distinctive ruby-red Aston Martin Volante sat in the prime spot closest to a door she suspected led directly to his office. She didn't attempt to confirm her guess. From this point forward, she'd need to play this very carefully, which meant entering the way everyone else did, through the front.

Opening a set of etched glass doors, she stepped into the foyer, taking a moment to absorb her surroundings. She'd never been here before, nor had she bothered to ask for a tour, in case Jack expected quid pro quo and felt he could or should ask about her job in return. She preferred not starting a conversation that might direct too much attention to her own work.

For some reason, the graciousness and Southern charm of the waiting area surprised her. It shouldn't. She'd seen his beach cottage—a misnomer if ever there were one since his Charleston home exuded wealth and contemporary luxury. And she'd also stayed at his home in Greenville, a sprawling plantation mansion that brilliantly blended the old South with the new.

At her entrance, the receptionist greeted her with a lovely smile. "Ms. Thomas?"

Nikki blinked in surprise. "That's right."

"Jack said to expect you. He bet me you'd show up right before closing." She laughed. "After all these years working for him, you'd think I'd know better than to bet against him. He has an uncanny knack for winning."

Nikki stifled a faint whiff of irritation. "So I've discovered," she said.

"Ah, clearly you know our Jack." *Our* Jack? "I'll show you to his office. He said you should go straight in."

She came around the reception desk and started down a wide hallway. Nikki pegged the woman to be in her mid-twenties, six or seven years younger than Nikki's own age. She wore a tidy pantsuit in a rich chocolate-brown that matched her eyes, her blond hair styled in a short, sassy cut that drew attention to her pretty features. She paused outside a set of double doors and gave a quick tap with her knuckle before swinging them open.

"Nikki Thomas to see you."

"Thanks, Lynn. You can shut down for the day."

"Okay. See you Monday." She offered Nikki another of her lovely smiles. "Nice meeting you, Ms. Thomas."

Jack glanced up from the file spread across his desk and gestured toward one of the chairs opposite him. The instant she sat, he crossed to the doors and closed them. For some reason the gesture struck her as ominous, adding to a vague dread that had been building all day.

Had it only been this morning when she'd woken to his mouth and body on hers? To the laughter and joy of their impromptu joining? To the delicious, mind-numbing aftermath? She closed her eyes at the memory, but couldn't seem to shut it down. Jack had carried her from their bed into the shower when the clock warned they'd be late for work if they didn't get up. Their shower together had prompted more laughter when they'd bumped and brushed their way clean.

And then had been the saucy moments when she'd dressed in the royal blue panties and bra set she was currently wearing. He'd joked about stripping away the bits and pieces she busily slipped on and suggested something that had brought a flush to her cheeks, while tempting her beyond bearing. Now she wished she'd taken him up on the offer since she doubted that opportunity would ever come again.

Without a word, Jack resumed his seat behind his desk—a captain at the helm of his ship. She shot him a swift, searching glance, but his expression remained closed to her. More than anything she wanted to break through the wall of ice separating them. But he was a master at closing his emotions behind thick barriers, no doubt a result of his unconventional upbringing. She knew from personal experience just how rarely he allowed others in, and just how badly he'd taken her betrayal.

In an attempt to distract herself, Nikki studied her surroundings. Like the waiting area, his office also reflected a graciousness overlaid with subtle hints of wealth and prosperity. No doubt it went a long way toward selling the various services Carolina Shipping offered its clients. It struck her as vastly different from TKG, where the rooms were appealing, but more functional in appearance, underscored with the strong masculine accent Reginald Kincaid had preferred.

The minutes ticked by and still neither of them spoke. Or perhaps the tension thickening the room spoke for them, whispering of pain and loss, secrets and deception. Unable to stand the building storm another instant, Nikki broke the silence, no doubt what Jack had intended all along.

"I'm sorry, Jack. I should have told you that I worked for the Kincaids right from the start." He didn't answer, just studied her with those unnerving pale blue eyes of his, the sheer lack of emotion ripping through her. She set the file folder she'd brought for him on the edge of his desk and nudged it in his direction. "I brought my reports, as requested."

His gaze flicked toward the folder then he stood again. This time he crossed to a wet bar and poured himself a drink. He glanced over his shoulder in her direction, lifting a dark eyebrow in clear question.

"No, thanks." Impatient with the continued silence, she said, "Are you going to say anything at all?"

"Hoping to get it over with quick and painless? Sorry, sweetheart. You're not getting off that easy."

She flinched at his sarcasm. Exhaustion dragged at her. It had been an endless day which would no doubt morph into an equally endless night. Thank God it was Friday and she'd have the entire weekend to come to terms with all that had happened today. "Jack, I made a mistake," she said in a low voice. "Are you really going to throw away what we have over a single omission?"

"What we have?" He took a long swallow of his drink. For the first time she caught a glimpse of his rage, the sheer depth and power of it leaving her shaken. "We *have* nothing. We *had*... Well, that's a different story."

Nikki blinked hard to hold back tears. "Please, Jack..."

"Don't." He slammed his drink against the wet bar, the cut glass tumbler singing in protest. "Just...don't."

"The Kincaids didn't know how serious our relationship had become. Nor did they ask me to do anything illegal or unethical."

Jack eyed her grimly. "You mean other than try to prove that I killed my father?"

Nikki shot to her feet. "Damn it, Jack. I know you didn't kill Reginald. I doubt the Kincaids even believe it of you. You could never do such a thing. You and your father might have had your differences, but I know what sort of man you are."

"And what sort of woman are you?"

"You know what sort."

His eyes chilled, growing colder than she'd ever seen them. "I do now."

Anger filled her, sweeping aside the tears. "I've never lied to you, Jack. Not about who I am or what's in my heart. Do you really believe I could have faked my reaction to your touch? To your kiss?" She dared to approach, part of her hoping to push through his self-control while the other part of her dreaded what might happen if she succeeded. "That I was pretending when you made love to me?"

Something fired in his eyes, flickering to life and melting through the chill that encased him. She stood within touching distance, a vulnerable spot to be in considering the depth of his sense of betrayal. Even prepared, his sudden lunge caught her by surprise. With a growl that hovered somewhere between fury and demand, he snatched her into his arms. And then he kissed her.

Where before he'd been winter-cold, now he exploded with blistering heat, taking without hesitation, claiming all she was and all she had. His mouth moved across hers in a passion laced with unmistakable pain. Her heart went out to him because she knew she'd caused that pain and would have given everything she possessed to ease it. She gave him free rein, offering herself to him unconditionally and without hesitation.

He didn't hold back, but she no longer cared. It had been like this from the start. From the first moment their eyes had met on a chilly winter evening while he'd been auctioned off before a crowd whose silence judged and ostracized him, there had been an irresistible spark. And later that evening when they'd talked, that spark had flickered into a flame, one that had leaped out of control the first time they touched. The first time they kissed—a kiss not that different from this one.

And when they'd gone on that initial date, her fate had been sealed. She could no more resist his pull than a wave could resist its tumbling journey to the shore. Even then she'd given him everything, despite the complications, knowing full well he was a man intent on destroying the Kincaids while Nikki was the one woman capable of stopping him.

Secrets. So many secrets.

Jack swept her into his arms and carried her to the sitting area of his office. There he lowered her to a plush sofa and followed her down. He kissed her again, slower this time, deeper, the passion thick and full and rich. She felt the slight tug and give of her suit jacket, followed by the cool wash of air across her skin before the heat of his hands replaced it, cupping her breasts through her bra.

"Show me that you want me," he said. "Prove to me that it wasn't an act."

Two

Nikki closed her eyes, the overwhelming desire of seconds before fading beneath Jack's clipped demand. "I have nothing to prove." She pushed at his shoulders, not certain whether she was relieved or disappointed when he pulled back. "Either you believe me or you don't. Either you believe in what we've felt for each other over the past four months or you don't. It's that simple."

"It's not that simple. You betrayed my trust." He sat up, allowing her room to swing her legs onto the floor. "But I still want you. God knows why."

"Gee, thanks."

"You spied on me, Nikki. I can't forgive that."

"And yet, you had no compunction asking me to spy on the Kincaids. Or is that somehow different?" She fumbled with her buttons, appalled to discover that her fingers trembled making the task nearly impossible.

"Here…let me." Sweeping her hands aside, he buttoned her jacket, realigning the buttons she'd shoved into the wrong holes. "First, I didn't ask you to spy on them. I asked you to investigate, which is quite different."

"How?" she asked. "Seriously, I'd love to know how you make that distinction."

"We were sleeping together while you were investigating me on the Kincaids' behalf. You aren't sleeping with the people I asked you to investigate." His eyes fixed on her. Narrowed. "Are you?"

She shot off the couch and spun to face him. Fury flowed through her and she didn't make any attempt to conceal the fact. "That's a filthy thing to suggest. You know Matt and RJ are both in committed relationships, on the verge of marriage. And just to be clear, I've never, ever had any sort of personal or intimate relationship with any of the Kincaids. Ever. I work for them. Period."

Something in her tone and ferocity must have gotten through to him. He inclined his head. "Okay, fine."

"No," she insisted. "It's not fine. You owe me an apology."

He stared at her with such an expression of disbelief it would have been amusing if the circumstances had been different. "Let me get this straight. *I* owe *you* an apology?"

She folded her arms across her chest. "You may recall that the first thing I did when I came here was apologize to you. I was in the wrong. I knew it and I said I was sorry. So, yes. You now owe me an apology for accusing me of sleeping with RJ and/or Matt."

"And/or?"

"Exactly. And, just for the record, I never slept with

your father, either. I think that covers all the Kincaid males, other than you."

"I never thought—" He broke off, his blue eyes turning even more stormy. "I'm not a Kincaid male."

She lifted her shoulder in a shrug. "Potato, pah-tah-toe. Apologize right this minute or I'm leaving."

"You're not leaving until we've had a chance to go over these reports of yours."

She simply lifted an eyebrow and waited.

"Son of a—" He scrubbed his hands over his face. "Okay, fine. I apologize. I shouldn't have accused you of sleeping with the Kincaids. But you were in bed with them, figuratively, if nothing else."

"I was working that entire time trying to prove your innocence." She closed her eyes and accepted the painful truth. "Except you're not innocent, are you?"

Jack slowly stood, anger rippling across his face. "What the hell does that mean? You just said you didn't believe I killed my father."

She waved that aside. "Of course you didn't."

"Then explain what you meant?"

"I mean that you plan to destroy everything your father spent his lifetime building." Unless someone stopped him. So many secrets. So many schemes. They wore her out, even though many of those secrets and schemes were resting in the palm of her own hand. She released her breath in an exhausted sigh. "Becoming involved with you was a mistake."

"News flash. I already figured that out."

She had to find a way to get through to him—other than this heartbreaking argument over her employers. They'd never see eye to eye on the subject. Nor did it get to the true heart of the problem—Jack's illogical vendetta against the Kincaids.

She dared take a step closer to him, seeing the wariness leap into his gaze, as well as a flash of something he struggled hard to conceal. Want. An irrepressible need that echoed the one sweeping through her. She moistened her lips and tried a new tack. "Jack, did you ever read the letter your father left you?"

She'd caught him off guard and his wariness grew. "No."

"He left one for each of his children. For your mother, too, from what I've heard. There must have been a reason for that. Something he wanted to say. Aren't you the least curious?"

"My relationship with my father was...complicated."

"Mine wasn't," she said simply.

"That's a bit cryptic. Care to explain?"

She hesitated. It wasn't a subject she liked talking about. It had caused a great deal of distress and pain in her life. But perhaps if he understood why she'd gone to work for TKG, he'd also understood why her loyalties were so torn. She forced herself to give it to him straight. "If it weren't for your father, I wouldn't have a career."

Jack shrugged. "Okay, so he gave you your start in the business."

"No, he didn't. I didn't even know him when I first started working."

"Then—"

"He helped me salvage my reputation after my previous employer ripped it to shreds." There. She'd said it. "He helped me out of a very tight corner."

A frown formed between Jack's dark brows. "What the hell happened?"

She hated discussing that time. Hated that she could have been so naive and foolish, especially considering her father had been a policeman and had drummed both caution and integrity into her practically from birth. But she hadn't been cautious. And the man she'd fallen in love with had lacked integrity, something that had ultimately rebounded on her.

She wished she'd accepted that drink when Jack first offered it, her mouth so bone-dry she felt as though she had to drag the words out from where they'd bottled in her throat. "It was my first real job after college, with newly minted degrees in police science and business administration."

"No one can accuse you of being an underachiever."

She smiled for the first time in what felt like days. "Did I mention my minor in criminal justice?"

"You did tell me you were considering going into law enforcement."

Her smile faded. "But I couldn't do that to my family, not when Dad went down in the line of duty. Instead, I made the classic mistake so many women do when they first start working."

It only took him a minute to make the leap. His uncanny knack for connecting the dots was one of the qualities she'd always appreciated about him. "You fell in love with your boss."

She couldn't help flinching. Hearing it stated so baldly made her aware of just how painfully young she'd been. How hopelessly inexperienced. "Yes. Even worse, he convinced me to keep our affair secret. He even proposed, promising that once we married, we could admit to the relationship. If my father had still been alive, I doubt it ever would have happened."

A hint of sympathy darkened Jack's gaze. "You did tell me he was an excellent judge of character."

"I thought I was, too." She paced the width of Jack's

office as though in an attempt to put distance between herself and those long-ago events. "I don't know. Maybe believing I was my father's daughter made me cocky."

Jack crossed to the wet bar, freshened his drink and poured her one, as well. "Here. I think you need this even more than I do."

She accepted the double malt scotch with a swift smile of gratitude and sipped, the rawness of the liquor catching in her throat and burning a warming path straight to her bones. Slowly she relaxed. "The details aren't really important. Let's just say Craig used my name for a land development scam he had going. When it all fell apart, he was long gone and I was left looking very, very guilty."

"How did my father end up involved?"

"Reginald was a close personal friend of my grandfather Beaulyn. Obviously, my mother's dad," she added.

Something swept across Jack's face, as though her grandfather's name rang a distant bell, and she froze, wondering if she'd made a terrible mistake mentioning his name. Then the moment passed. "But your father was a cop. I'm surprised the Beaulyns would have encouraged the match."

Nikki shrugged. "My parents met at college. It didn't matter that they came from different social backgrounds. Mom always claimed it was love at first sight. When I had my issues with Craig, your father felt he owed my grandfather and stepped in to help me."

"Explain that."

As much as she wished she could tell Jack the whole truth, the time had come to tiptoe. "Grandpa was a very savvy businessman who made an impressive amount of money in real estate. He was also old money, part of the upper echelons of Charleston's social elite."

Jack's eyes narrowed. "Which would have attracted Dad. One of the reasons he married Elizabeth was to penetrate Charleston's old-money bastions. Apparently new money didn't smell as good to them as old."

She suspected he spoke from current, personal experience and couldn't help remembering the charity auction where he'd been so soundly snubbed—right up until she'd bid for him. "I'm not in a position to argue the point. The bottom line is, Reginald caught wind of it, possibly through my mother. He stepped in and salvaged my reputation. Then he hired me to work for The Kincaid Group."

"So you feel you owe him."

"I do owe him, Jack," Nikki replied steadily. "Your father had his flaws, I won't pretend otherwise. But he also had quite a few strengths, most of which you've inherited. And there's no doubt in my mind that he loved his children—all of them."

"I assume that brings us back to the letter he left me."

She nodded. "Aren't you curious about why your father left you such a large percentage of TKG? Why he divided the other forty-five percent between RJ, Matt, Laurel, Lily and Kara?"

"No."

Okay, so that utter black-and-white quality was one of the characteristics she wished he hadn't inherited from Reginald. "All that matters is that he's given you the means to gain control of The Kincaid Group?" she demanded. "Offered you the opportunity to take revenge on your brothers and sisters?"

"They're not my brothers and sisters." Emotion ripped apart his words.

"Of course they are. And they've done nothing to

you, Jack. They didn't even know you existed until shortly after your father's death."

His mouth tightened. "They didn't exactly welcome us with open arms."

Oh, for… "Would you have in their place?" she asked in exasperation.

Jack made an impatient gesture. "Why are we even discussing this? You were supposed to come here in order to discuss your reports. Instead, we've done everything but."

"I hoped I could get you to see what a difficult position I'm in. What a difficult position we're all in because of Reginald's actions. The Kincaids want me to investigate you. You want me to investigate them…."

"Actually, I asked you to uncover the identity of the person or persons who own the remaining ten percent of TKG stock. Have you even bothered looking?" He broke off, the muscles along his jaw tightening. "Son of a bitch…"

Uh-oh. "Jack—"

His eyes narrowed and anger flickered to life in his eyes again. "You are looking, aren't you? Only it's for them. RJ's already asked you to find the missing shareholder because whoever controls them, wins control of the company. That's why you've been stringing me along all this time, so RJ can get to this person ahead of me and have them squarely in his corner before the annual board meeting."

Nikki allowed Jack's words to hang in the air, hoping against hope that he'd take them back. When it became clear that he wouldn't, she crossed to the doors of his office. She paused for a brief moment then turned. "You know, as much as I loved and admired your father, there was one quality about him I could never come to terms with. For such a caring, generous person, he was one of the most ruthless men I've ever met, especially when it came to achieving his own ends. It's a shame you've decided to emulate him in that regard."

And with that, she exited his office. She hadn't thought she could feel any worse than when she'd first arrived. But she did.

What was she going to do now? A battle was brewing between the Kincaids and Jack, one growing progressively more dangerous and messy. It only required a single spark for open warfare to erupt. Unfortunately, she was that spark.

Because as soon as either side discovered she owned those final ten percent shares of Kincaid stock, they would all come gunning for her.

How the hell had she done it?

Swearing beneath his breath, Jack snatched up the file Nikki had left on his desk. How had she managed to turn the tables on him so completely? *He'd* been wronged—by *her*. All this time she'd been working for the enemy, gathering God knows what information for his brothers and sisters—*not* his brothers and sisters, he swiftly corrected himself, but those damn Legitimates. And why? To use against him, that's why. And then she had the unmitigated gall to stare at him with those big sapphire-blue eyes all full of hurt and reproach as though *he* were the one at fault.

Well, he refused to buy into it. She should have told him the truth right from the start.

And if she had? What would he have done?

He swore again and dropped into his chair. Would he have attempted to turn her against her employers? Would he have bribed her? Used their relationship to have her go against her ethics, an ethical code instilled by the father she so adored? He didn't want to think he'd sink so low, but then, how rational was his need for revenge against the Kincaids?

Worse, she'd been appallingly right. He was every bit as ruthless as Reginald Kincaid; his entire life was dedicated to the pursuit of eclipsing the company his father had spent a lifetime building. Jack forced himself to stare unflinchingly at his motivations for creating Carolina Shipping and winced. It wasn't a pretty picture. He'd been his father's firstborn and had been denied that birthright thanks to circumstances beyond his control. As a result, he'd been determined to prove himself better and more capable than any of his father's other sons—for once in his life to be first and receive acknowledgment of that fact.

With his father gone, that would never happen.

Jack tipped his head back against the leather headrest and sighed. Great. Just great. Score one for Nikki. All these years he'd managed to remain delightfully oblivious to the underlying cause for his drive to succeed. Even more, he'd have been quite content to remain oblivious until the day he'd succeeded in taking over TKG. Now, even that was denied him, and all thanks to Nikki Thomas, the one woman in all creation he'd come within an inch of falling in love with.

And then there was the story she'd told him about her first job. About Craig. She'd been used once before and badly burned. Had she kept her silence about her job out of concern he'd use her the way Craig had? Granted, different circumstances, but still… Jack straightened in his chair and faced another unpalatable truth—score two for Nikki.

If he'd discovered she worked for the Kincaids,

chances were excellent he'd have used their relationship to try and turn her. The knowledge left a bitter taste in his mouth. Even worse, he'd been one short step away from attempting to put pressure on her tonight in order to find that missing shareholder. To somehow force her to give him the identity before turning the information over to RJ. What the hell had happened to him? And how the hell could he fix the situation?

When no easy answer presented itself, he flipped open the file and read through every word Nikki had written. He couldn't fault it. The report was concise, accurate and utterly unbiased, even the part that reported that his Aston Martin had been parked in a lot near TKG the night of his father's murder. God only knew how that was possible, since he'd left it in the parking lot of Carolina Shipping when he'd arrived at work and it was still there when he left.

The one detail which caught him off guard he found in a short addendum advising RJ Kincaid that her father, Peter Thomas, had been partners with the lead detective assigned to the murder case. That would be Charles McDonough. Jack grimaced. He'd met the man and might have liked him if the circumstances surrounding their meeting had been different. But being interviewed by the detective was not conducive to a budding friendship.

Jack returned his attention to the file. He didn't find any information that Nikki could have learned only as a result of their affair, and nowhere else. All of her facts were documented and annotated, with referenced sources. She'd have made an excellent cop, despite the fact that her family had put pressure on her to choose a different career after her father had gone down in the line of duty. Jack wished he could have known Peter

Thomas since he suspected the apple hadn't fallen far from that particular tree.

Then he had another, even more uncomfortable thought. What would Thomas have thought of him? Would he have lumped Jack in with Craig and warned his daughter to end their relationship? Quite likely. Jack shoved aside the file with a sigh. And didn't that just bite.

What was it about Nikki that forced him to take such a long, hard look at his own character—and find it lacking? He was honest, hardworking, generous. Okay, ruthless, hardheaded, driven. But for the past four months they'd been perfect for each other. Right up until those damn Kincaids got in the way again. Jack shoved back his chair. Well, he knew what he had to do and the sooner he got it over with the better.

It didn't take long to drive to Rainbow Row where Nikki owned one of the historic homes, an inheritance from her grandfather she'd once told him. And though she'd told him the night of the auction that she came from Charleston's elite on her mother's side, she'd neglected to mention it was the illustrious Beaulyn family. No doubt she was concerned that such a stellar connection would cause friction between them considering his general animosity toward high society. Still, the name rang a distant bell, and for more than its social significance.

Jack approached Nikki's door and debated knocking, then decided against it since he found it highly doubtful she'd let him in. Instead, he used the key she'd given him. He paused in the foyer, his gaze inevitably going to the stretch of wall where they'd collided while in the throes of their second kiss—an innocent embrace that had unexpectedly burst into a storm of desperate need.

It had been a continuation of the first kiss they'd shared on the night of the charity auction. From that incendiary start, the affair had swiftly taken off, flaming higher and higher over the past three months.

Right until it had crashed and burned this morning.

"Nikki?" he called out.

He heard swift footsteps coming from the general direction of the kitchen. A second later Nikki appeared. She'd changed from her business suit into some sort of light, filmy cover-up. He remembered it from one of the occasions when she'd spent the night at his beach house. It had been no more than a brief glimpse all those weeks ago, just the amount of time it took to see the tantalizing way it clung to her lush figure and the additional few seconds it took to strip it off her.

She paused a dozen feet away from him and stared for an endless moment, her eyes black in the dusky light. His expression must have given her some clue as to why he was there. With a small exclamation, she flew into his arms.

He held her tight, catching himself inhaling her unique fragrance, as though stamping it onto some primal memory that told him that this was his mate, the only woman who would ever be his mate. "I'm sorry," he murmured. She simply shook her head, burrowing against him. It took him a split second to realize she was crying. "Oh, God, don't, Nikki. I'm so sorry."

When she still didn't answer, he swept her into his arms and carried her upstairs to her bedroom. After toeing off his shoes, he climbed into bed with her and simply held her against his chest until she finished weeping.

"You okay now?" he asked gently, brushing back her fringe of bangs and kissing her forehead.

She ducked her head. "Don't look at me. I'm not

one of those sweet Southern belles who cries without smudging their makeup. I'm one of those whose nose turns red and runny and whose face gets all blotchy. Mother blames my Thomas blood since apparently a Beaulyn wouldn't dare do the ugly cry."

His mouth twitched in amusement. "So noted. I'm now too terrified to look."

To his relief a small hiccupped laugh escaped. "Okay, now I have to know." A hint of tension rippled through body. "Why are you here, Jack?"

"Do I really have to say it?"

He despised postmortems after an argument. How many of them had he been privy to whenever his parents fought and reconciled? Too many to count, their passion loud and messy, spilling over onto those too close to escape. No wonder he and Alan were so screwed up, though in totally opposite ways. His Sinclair half brother had always been appalled by the excess of emotion—emotion their mother, Angela, had never shared with Alan's father, Richard Sinclair.

Had Alan resented that fact? Jack had never considered the possibility before. Considering how protective Alan was toward their mother, the likelihood existed, despite the loving relationship he claimed to share with Jack's father, Reginald Kincaid. While Alan clung tighter to his parental relationships, Jack had closed himself off from others, building a protective wall around his emotions. Refusing to allow others to stir the sort of intemperate passion his parents shared, a passion that had destroyed so many lives.

Nikki released a long sigh, interrupting his musings. "Did you expect to waltz in here after everything that happened today and just pick up where we left off?"

He winced at the stinging note in her voice. "Expect? No. Hope? You're damn right I did."

"Jack."

"Okay, you want to hear it again? I'm sorry."

She peeked up at him through damp, spiky lashes. "Why are you sorry?" she asked suspiciously.

"I'm afraid—seriously afraid—that I might be like Craig," he confessed.

Nikki must not have anticipated that particular answer. She pulled back another couple of inches, confirming that she'd been dead serious about her crying jags. She wasn't a pretty crier. For some reason, it endeared her to him all the more. "Craig?" she asked in confusion. "You're nothing like Craig."

"I'm not sure your father would agree." He brooded over it for another moment. "I suspect if you told me you worked for TKG, I'd have used our relationship to convince you to spy on the Kincaids."

Her eyes narrowed a trifle, a steely gleam glittering through her tears. "FYI, you wouldn't have succeeded."

"Don't be so sure." He deliberately feathered his hand along her cheek and down the length of her neck, eliciting a helpless shiver. "I can be pretty persuasive when I choose."

She gave herself a little shake and pulled back farther still as though a few more inches of distance would improve her chances of resisting him. He'd have laughed if not for the hint of shrewdness in her gaze. "Just out of curiosity, what information would you have had me turn over to you?"

The question caught him totally off guard. Okay, so maybe his powers of persuasion were on the fritz. They certainly seemed to be tonight. "I don't know. Information I could use to gain control of The Kincaid Group."

"Jack, the only way you can gain control of TKG is if you also control the majority of the shares. The same goes for RJ. And since you asked me to find out who the missing shareholder is when you didn't know I worked for the Kincaids, and that's the same information you'd have wanted if you *did* know I worked for the Kincaids, I don't see how you could have used me."

It took him a moment to work through her reply. "Convoluted, but true," he conceded. "But what if I'd asked you to give me any defamatory information about RJ or Matt or one of their sisters? Information I could have used against them at the annual meeting?"

"I'd have said no," she retorted with a hint of exasperation. "Besides, there is no defamatory information. Jack, your brothers and sisters are nice people. If you'd only give them a chance you'd discover that for yourself."

His jaw set. "I have no intention of discovering that for myself."

"Oh, Jack." It was her turn to shift closer, to stroke a gentle hand along his raspy cheek. For some reason her powers of persuasion were working much better than his, damn it. "They're as innocent in all this as you are."

"That doesn't change their attitude toward me."

"Their father had just been murdered, a man they'd loved and respected all their lives," she shot right back. "A man they thought they knew as well as they knew themselves. Instead of being able to mourn him, they're faced with the news that he's been keeping a second family hidden away. That the pillar of Charleston society has feet of clay. It takes time to come to terms with that."

"They've had five months," he insisted stubbornly.

"Jack, they're no more responsible for the family dynamics than you are. Your life and how you were forced to spend it was your mother and father's responsibility. They're the ones who should be held accountable, not your brothers and sisters."

He was being unreasonable and knew it. That didn't change the fact that he'd lived his entire life in the shadows, had never known the acceptance his Kincaid kin had experienced from the moment they'd entered the world, all because he'd had the misfortune to be born a bastard. For years he'd competed head-to-head with The Kincaid Group, fighting and clawing for each and every sale, while his brothers had been handed their positions on a silver platter. Soon all that would change. Soon they'd be forced to answer to him. That moment couldn't come any too soon. Nor would it be any too sweet.

Nikki sighed, breaking the silence growing between them. "All I'm saying is that you might consider giving them a chance."

"Fine." He dismissed his relatives without the least hesitation. "Next problem."

"The missing shares," she said unhappily.

She keyed in on the remaining issue standing between them with unerring accuracy. He'd always admired her focus and logic, even if it was all too often coated with an unfortunate sentimentality.

He nodded. "Eventually you're going to find out who owns them, Nikki. How will you handle the information when you do?"

"To be honest, I don't know," she confessed.

"At the very least I hope you'll give both RJ and me the information at the same time so neither of us has an unfair advantage."

She wiggled against him, confirming how uncomfortable the subject made her. She'd always been that way about it, even before he'd discovered she worked for the Kincaids. Invariably, she'd change the topic whenever it came up in casual conversation. He'd always assumed it wasn't something that interested her. Now he realized it struck too close to home.

"I'll think about it," she finally conceded.

He'd have to be satisfied with that. "I have one more request."

"I'm almost afraid to ask…."

He caught the wary tone in her voice and suspected he'd pushed her about as far as she'd be pushed. Still, this was important. More than important. "I read through the reports you brought to my office. They were excellent, by the way. Very fair and accurate."

"Thanks. I try."

He winced at the chill that iced her words. "I noticed that Charles McDonough was your father's former partner."

She confirmed it with a quick nod. "Our families have maintained a close friendship. What's this about, Jack? What do you want?"

Time for dead honesty. "I need to clear my name," he stated tersely. "And I need you to help me do it."

Three

Nikki's expression softened. "Jack, I know you didn't kill your father. I wouldn't be in bed with you if I had the least doubt."

"You're the only one who doesn't have the least doubt." He yanked at his tie to loosen the knot. For some reason it threatened to choke him. "The police are looking my way. McDonough has already interviewed me a couple of times. I have a feeling I'm his most likely suspect."

"Looking is a long way from arresting you for the crime and even further from convicting you." But she sounded uneasy.

"I understand all that. Right now the evidence is barely circumstantial. My car parked near TKG the night of the murder is hardly persuasive evidence. That doesn't change the fact that someone killed my father. I want you to help me find out who. Or if we can't find out the actual identity of the murderer, at least help me prove it wasn't me."

She shook her head. "I can't and won't interfere with an ongoing police investigation. Charles may be a close family friend, but he won't tolerate that, not even from me," she warned.

"I'm not asking you to interfere. Nikki…your reports were brilliant." When she started to deny it, he stopped her. "No, truly. They were logical, careful, thorough. You have a very analytical mind and a knack for sifting through large amounts of data and extracting key nuggets of information. I need that sort of help."

She gave a helpless shrug. "I don't know what you think I can uncover that the police can't."

"I don't know if it's that they can't or if they simply choose not to, at least not when they have a convenient suspect at hand."

"Oh, no, Jack." She rolled onto her hip to face him and cupped his face. "Charles isn't like that, not at all."

He planted a kiss in the palm of her hand, the gesture taking on a symbolic feel. "The Kincaids would be delighted to have the police pin my dad's murder on me," he said. "In fact, I wouldn't be surprised if they weren't nudging McDonough in my direction. Not only would it take care of the problems I'm causing at TKG, it also sweeps the bastard son out of sight so the Kincaids can pretend I never existed."

"First, Charles can't be nudged. If he could, he'd never have arrested Reginald's wife for the murder. It wasn't until Elizabeth allowed Cutter Reynolds to step forward and admit that she was with him that night at the time of the murder—that they'd been having an affair for three years—that she was released."

Jack reluctantly nodded. "Fair enough. That doesn't

change the fact that over the past five months the suspect pool has gotten smaller and smaller. Hell, right
now it's barely a puddle and I'm the only one left splash-
ing around in it. I flat-out refuse to sit around and wait
for them to find some trumped-up piece of evidence
with which to hang me. Even if you refuse to help, I
plan to look into this on my own."

Nikki frowned. "You're not giving me much choice,
Jack."

"It's the Craig coming out in me."

To his relief, her frown eased then evaporated like
morning fog hovering over the Cooper River. "You will
never be like Craig," she informed him.

She spoke with such tenderness that it left him
speechless…though not motionless. Gently, he pulled
her into his arms and kissed her. His mouth drifted
across hers, slow and easy. He nibbled at her bottom
lip, running his tongue along the seam before dipping
inward for a leisurely taste.

"Have I ever told you that you have the most perfect
lips of any woman I've ever kissed?"

Her smile melded with the kiss. "Do I?"

"Mmm. They're just the right size and shape. Plump
without suffocating a man. Wide without swallowing
a man whole."

Her laughter rang out. "Heaven forbid."

"And best of all they're clever. Very, very clever, just
like the woman who possesses them."

"Well, allow me to return the compliment. I just
happen to think that not only are your lips perfect, but
so is the way you use them." She ran a finger along his
mouth, giving his bottom lip a little pinch similar to
the nibbling bite he'd given hers. "Unlike some men

who are long forgotten, you don't just dive in and attack my mouth."

For some reason his voice deepened, turning rough and gravelly. "I seem to remember attacking it a time or two."

"Only when the occasion called for it," she assured him. "The rest of the time you start slow and teasing, and oh, so tempting. Like this…" She gave him a vivid demonstration, one that had his mind clouding over and blood pooling in an area of his body nowhere near his mouth. "And then you slip in, like the sun slipping from the ocean and turning everything golden. You steal my breath, Jack. I don't understand how or why, but you do. And then you give me yours so I can breathe again."

He closed his eyes, more moved than he could ever remember. "Nikki…"

"Make love to me, Jack. Steal my breath and turn my world golden again."

Jack didn't need any further prompting. Rearing back, he knelt above Nikki and stripped away his suit coat and tie. The buttons of his shirt proved beyond his ability to manipulate and he dealt with them in the easiest possible way. He ripped his shirt open and tossed it aside, while she tackled his trousers, her hands as clumsy as his own in her haste to deal with his belt buckle and zipper. Though it seemed endless, it couldn't have been longer than a minute before all he wore was skin. And then he turned his attention to Nikki.

Her cover-up was a pale gleam, the color indeterminate, in the dimness of the bedroom. Beneath it she wore the royal blue bra and panties he'd had the pleasure of watching her slip on just that morning. Now he'd have the greater pleasure of removing them. He caught the hem of the semitransparent scrap of silk in his hands and drew it up and off.

She emerged, a bit more rumpled, but infinitely more beautiful. She'd let her hair down after she left his office and it flowed to her shoulders in an ebony curtain, the ends curving inward to cup her shoulders. The darkness of the color made a delicious contrast to her pearlescent skin, giving a richness to the sepia overtones. She fell back against the pillows and offered her siren's smile, a silent promise of pleasures to come.

For a split second, time froze, tilted. From the moment he'd first seen Nikki at the Read and Write auction, striding across the grounds of the Colonel Samuel Beauchamp House, her lean, shapely figure encased in form-fitting black wool, he'd wanted her. And when she'd paused to stare up at where he stood on a balcony overlooking the impeccably landscaped backyard and patio, he'd desired her with a ferocity he'd never experienced with any other woman.

She'd stood so fearlessly beneath him, gazing up with those stunning sapphire eyes and then she'd shocked him by bidding, offering a thousand dollars for the pleasure of his company for one night of dinner and dancing, when all those around her had refused to make a single offer, despite the fact that the event was for charity. Even more fascinating, she'd demanded an additional incentive—a single wish to be collected at a time of her choosing. She never collected on that wish, though he didn't doubt she would at some point. But he'd collected their very first kiss that same night, tracking her down and pulling her into his arms, driven to put his stamp of possession on her.

Instead, she'd put hers on him.

Ever since that first kiss he'd been connected to her

in a way he didn't understand and couldn't begin to explain. The depths of his feelings bothered him, perhaps because they were too close an echo of what he suspected his father felt for his mother. Worse, it disturbed the even tenor of his life, upset the clear-cut goals he'd set for himself. Disrupted the urges that had driven him for most of his life. She made him question himself, to look far too closely at his motivations. And he didn't like it. Not that his displeasure changed a thing. He still wanted her with a desperation he couldn't deny or sate.

"What's wrong?" Nikki asked, her voice soft and gentle, filled with a perceptiveness that arrowed straight through to the core of who and what he was.

"You have a knack for knocking me off balance and keeping me there." The words were dragged from him with an unwillingness he couldn't disguise.

"Should I apologize?" she asked gravely.

"Yes."

"A shame since I quite like having you off balance."

As though to prove her point, she took his hand in hers and gave it a yank, catching him by surprise. He fell forward, supporting his weight with hands he braced on either side of her head. "You're trouble," he informed her. "I knew it when you bid for me."

"You're mine. I made sure of it when I won you." She tugged at his shoulders, pulling him downward so skin pressed intimately to skin. She hesitated, her expression turning unusually serious. "I would never betray you, Jack. I want you to know that."

"Your reports proved that," he replied just as seriously. "There were a few details you could have included that you didn't."

"What sort of details?"

"Over the past three months I've mentioned various

new business contracts up for grabs. You could have reported those to the Kincaids."

Her brows drew together. "How do you know I didn't? I could have told them in person. After all, it would have been foolish to leave a paper trail."

"Even so, you didn't, otherwise I wouldn't have won the contracts."

"That doesn't prove—"

"I would have lost a few of them, probably more than a few, if you'd told the Kincaids about it. Not only that, but on at least two occasions you had access to my bid sheets, if you'd been so inclined to pass on the information."

"I wasn't so inclined," she replied, a tart edge sliding through her words.

"I'm well aware of that." He touched her hair in a reconciliatory manner. "Why are we arguing about this when there are so many more interesting things we could be doing?"

She shook her head. "I don't know. Okay, yes, I do." She caught his face between her hands and lifted upward to kiss him, a slow, soothing kiss that promised they'd soon be getting to every last one of those "interesting things."

"I just want to make it clear that no matter what happens in the future, I would never betray you."

The words held an ominous undertone, one he refused to dwell on. Not when he held a naked woman in his arms. "I appreciate the reassurance."

Before she could say anything else, he cupped her breast and took a loving bite from the apple. Her breath exploded from her lungs and she moaned in pleasure. "Again. Do that again."

Instead, he turned his attention to her other breast,

teasing the nipple with his tongue, allowing the warmth of his exhale to fan the dampness. She shuddered at the teasing sensation, moving restlessly beneath him, the friction adding to the tension building between them. He never tired of reacquainting himself with all that made her so deliciously female, her curves generous where they should be generous and delicate where they should be delicate. He waited until he felt the slight give to her muscles signaling her relaxation and then used his teeth to tug at her nipple again.

With an incoherent cry, she arched beneath him, her hands sliding into his hair and holding him close to her breast. Unable to resist, his hands skated downward, tripping across the toned ripple of her abdomen to the joining between her thighs. She opened to him and he cupped her warmth, reveling in skin so soft it defied comparison. And still, he teased, finding the moist seam that hid the feminine core of her at the same instant as his tongue penetrated the moist seam of her mouth.

She went under, dragging him with her, surging upward with her hips while she rolled with him until she lay on top. She was incandescent in her want, beautiful and determined, more giving than any woman he'd known. Her hands swept down his chest and she broke the kiss to follow the path of her hands, mimicking all he'd done to her earlier. Her breath came hot against his skin, her mouth and teeth avid against his own nipples.

And all the while her hands were busy, busy, busy, finding the source of his own desire and stoking it to the level of a raging inferno. Just when he didn't think he could take it another instant, she eased down onto him, enclosing him in searing heat. She paused for an eternity like some sort of pagan goddess, her head thrown back, her rich, dark hair cascading down her back. Then she moved, setting in motion the first steps to a dance she'd come close to perfecting in the three months they'd been together.

He grasped her hips, moving with her, leading then following until there were no leaders. No followers. Just two people melded together so completely, their movements and desires so in tune with one another, that for a moment he thought they were one. One body. One need. One thought. One emotion.

The dance swirled faster and faster until it could go no further. With a hoarse cry, Jack thrust upward, reaching for Nikki, pulling her close. He felt her shatter a split second before he followed her over, the tumble endless and endlessly satisfying. Gasping for breath, she collapsed against him, a boneless melting that would have had him laughing if only he had sufficient air.

He wrapped his arms around her and held her close, her name the only word he was capable of uttering. She pressed a kiss to his damp chest, delicious little shudders sweeping through her in the aftermath of their lovemaking. "I keep thinking it can't get any better," she murmured. "And you keep proving me wrong."

"I do my best," he said humbly.

He felt her smile against his chest. "Now be quiet and go to sleep."

"I thought that was supposed to be my line."

Her soft laugh rumbled straight through him. "Since I was on top this time, my line."

Jack was asleep before the smile faded from his face.

Nikki woke to the deepness of night, disoriented by the hard masculine body beneath her own. She shifted, realizing to her amusement that Jack slept soundly on his stomach while she lay draped across his back like a human blanket, his firm male buttocks cushioning her hips. Her soft chuckle caused him to stir beneath her.

"What the hell…?"

"Apparently, I've turned kinky in my sleep," she commented.

"I'd agree with you, except there's not much either of us can do in this position."

She gave his rump an appreciative pat. "Speak for yourself." Rolling off him, she sat up and blinked sleepily at the digital clock. The soft blue glow informed her it was almost two and the dinner she'd been in the middle of preparing when Jack arrived had gone uneaten. "Man, I'm starving. What about you?"

"I could choke down a steak if you forced me." He levered upward. "Along with the rest of the cow, right down to the hide, hooves and tail."

She wrinkled her nose. "Not so sure about the hide and hooves, not to mention the tail, but I do have a nice big steak with your name on it. It won't take a minute to grill."

"Lead the way."

Nikki retrieved her cover-up on the way out of the room, ignoring Jack's sleepy protest. "I'm not cooking naked. There are too many parts I might burn."

"That silky thing isn't much protection," he informed her, pulling on his trousers.

"Not from you, maybe, but it's protection enough from any cooking spatter."

Fortunately, she managed to avoid the spatter. She didn't even attempt to avoid Jack's occasional caress. Why would she, when they were so delicious? It didn't take long to pull together a quick meal, especially with Jack's help. His willingness to lend a hand in the kitchen—or anywhere else she needed it—was one of the things that had impressed her right from the start.

He exuded a tough, masculine competence, going about his chores with a calm ease and economy of motion that spoke of a man comfortable in his own skin. And despite the ruthlessness she'd accused him of inheriting from his father, he also possessed unlimited generosity toward others, as well as a deep-seated tenderness that came out at the most unexpected times. Of equal importance to her, he possessed an innate honesty that tempered that ruthless streak. It reminded her of her father and it saddened her that the two men would never know each other since she suspected they'd have been firm friends.

Though Nikki had turned on a few lights, the denseness of night invaded the house, adding an air of intimacy to the process. As soon as the meal was prepared, she carried it to an alcove off the kitchen where a small café table and chairs were placed for more informal meals. Aside from the overhead spots, darkness enclosed them like a cozy blanket.

Silence prevailed while they made inroads into their meal. After several moments, Jack shot her a direct look, regarding her with a calmness she often associated with his business face. "It occurs to me that you never answered my question earlier."

"What question is that?"

As he so often did, he answered with absolute directness. "Will you help me look into the murder of my father?"

She hesitated, recalling his warning that he intended to pursue it regardless of whether or not she chose to help. She didn't doubt his sincerity for a single moment. Nor did she doubt that his single-minded drive might lead him to places better avoided. Maybe if she were there to temper his actions, they'd both manage to circumvent trouble.

"I'm willing to help…with a few conditions."

He tackled his steak once again, a small smile tugging at his mouth. "Why doesn't that surprise me?"

"First, I won't do anything that harms the Kincaids or interferes with my job there."

Jack shook his head. "I can't promise that, Nikki. What if one of them killed Dad?"

"Obviously, that's a different story."

"If that's the case, then you'll have to be willing to look long and hard at them, to give serious consideration to the possibility that someone you like, someone you care about, could be the murderer."

"It's not them," she replied steadily. "Just as I know it's not you, I know that none of your brothers and sisters would kill their own father, any more than you would."

He leveled her with a hard look. "Stop referring to them that way. They're not my brothers and sisters."

"Alan's also a half brother and yet I've heard you call him your brother."

"Only when forced to," Jack replied unenthusiastically.

She couldn't help laughing. Not that she blamed him. Alan was…odd. Though charming and easy on the eyes, he seemed to dislike the sort of hard work that the Kincaids thrived on. And that included Jack, who she considered a Kincaid by blood, if not by name.

In looks, Alan took after his and Jack's mother, Angela. They both shared the same golden-blond hair and lively hazel eyes. But while Angela possessed an underlying grit and determination, despite a distinctive air of vulnerability, Alan simply conveyed weakness and the general attitude that the world owed him a living. Even when offered that living, as Reginald had in his will—requesting a position be made available for Alan at The Kincaid Group—not once in the past five months had Alan followed through.

"To get back to the point of the conversation, I have another condition which is that we can't interfere in the police investigation in any way," Nikki continued. "I won't put Charles in an awkward position or do anything to compromise his case."

"Agreed. Anything else?"

"I don't think so."

The words had scarcely left her lips before Jack leaned forward and gave her a swift kiss. "That seals our deal."

"Knowing you, I'd better reserve the right to add the occasional addendum to our agreement."

He shook his head. "Too late. You're welcome to try to add something else but I can't promise I'll agree to it."

"You're a tough man to bargain with."

"Hey, I was cutting you some slack."

"If that's cutting me slack, I'd hate to see when you're negotiating in earnest."

For a split second his expression altered, allowing her to catch a glimpse of the business predator he rarely revealed to her. A chill shot down her spine. Heaven help her, but she hoped she'd never have cause to face him across the negotiating table. Jack was a man who played for keeps and she'd do well to remember that. She hadn't realized it at the time, but he'd let her off the hook over today's fiasco with relative ease. It would have been far different if he'd been just a hair more ruthless, more unforgiving or hadn't given a damn about maintaining their relationship.

Then another thought struck, one she forced herself to dismiss, but suspected would linger in the far recesses of her mind for some time to come. What if he had another purpose for reconciling with her tonight? What if it had only been because he still needed her...versus he cared about their relationship more than his vendetta against the Kincaids or his desire to clear his name?

Jack paused in the process of clearing their plates from the table. "What's wrong?" he asked. "You look upset."

Nikki shook her head, avoiding his gaze. "It's nothing."

She forced out a smile and pitched in to help with the dishes. She was wrong. She had to be. Jack wouldn't use her like that. She spared him a swift glance.

Would he?

The two slept in Saturday morning, curled together so completely Nikki couldn't tell where she left off and where Jack began.

"So, what's our first move?" he asked after they'd polished off a light brunch.

She hesitated. "You're handing me the lead?"

"Sure, why not?" A quick smile came and went. "I'm not such a control freak that I don't know how and when to delegate. You can't build a top-notch company without that ability. I also know how to choose the best person for any given job. And for this job, you're it."

"Okay. I can handle it." Maybe. She gave it a moment's thought and realized the first step was fairly obvious. "We should visit Elizabeth."

Jack frowned and she could guess why. While the

Kincaids would consider Angela Sinclair "the other woman," for most of Jack's life Elizabeth held that position in the Sinclair household. Considering how protective he was of his mother, she didn't doubt he resented Elizabeth and her claim to the Kincaid name.

"Why do we have to see her?" he asked reluctantly.

"We don't if it'll be too difficult for you." She shifted closer, offering her warmth and comfort. "She's the most stressful of the Kincaids for you to deal with, isn't she?"

He hesitated, on the verge of denying it, before inclining his head. "She possessed what my mother spent most of her life craving. His name. Recognition. Acceptance. When I was younger, I would have given anything and everything to provide Mom with that. But it wasn't in my power."

"Nor was it Elizabeth's fault," Nikki said gently.

"Logically, I know that. But emotionally…" He shook his head.

"So, you hate her."

"Actually, I don't," he surprised Nikki by admitting. "It took most of my teenage years to get to the point where I could see what my parents were doing to her was wrong, dead wrong, not the other way around. She was the injured party, not either of my parents." He gave a quick shrug. "That doesn't change the protectiveness I feel toward my mother."

Nikki hugged him close, relieved when he returned the hug. She could practically see another barrier between them fading into nonexistence. "Of course it doesn't change how you feel about your mother. And it shouldn't."

"So, why do we have to meet with Elizabeth?"

"Other than the killer, she was the last person to see

your father alive. I think it's worth talking to her about what happened that night."

He took a split second to consider then nodded. "That's logical. Why don't you phone her. Somehow I think she'll be more willing to agree to a meet if the request comes from you."

She placed the call, not the least surprised when it took several minutes to convince Elizabeth to speak with them about Reginald's death. Nikki could understand her reluctance and desire to put that night behind her. But finally they agreed to meet at Maybelle's, a coffeehouse not far from Rainbow Row. She and Jack arrived first and arranged for a table toward the back, well away from the general flow of traffic. They didn't have long to wait before the widow put in an appearance. To their surprise, her fiancé, Cutter Reynolds, was with her.

She swept up to the table, aggression sparking in her distinctive green eyes and communicating itself in the tense way she held her elegant body. Though Nikki knew for a fact that Elizabeth Kincaid celebrated her sixtieth birthday this year, she remained a stunning woman, looking a full decade younger than her chronological age. She wore her auburn hair cut in a short, trendy style and had kept her figure trim, her athletic build showcased by an off-white pair of slacks and bronze silk blouse. Discreet bits of gold flashed at her ears, wrists and neck.

"I don't know what you want from me, but I doubt there's anything I can say to help you," she announced, lobbing the first volley.

Jack stood and regarded her for a long moment, then held out his hand. "Even so, I appreciate your joining us, Mrs. Kincaid, especially considering I must represent a living insult to you and your marriage."

She stared at his hand for a long moment. Behind her, Cutter murmured her name and just like that her anger slipped away. With a soft sigh, she took Jack's hand and gave it a firm shake. "Oh, for heaven's sake, call me Elizabeth. As if all this wasn't awkward enough." To Nikki's surprise she gave a short huff of exasperation. "And fool that I am, here I have us meeting in public where everyone can see and gossip about it."

Jack nodded in perfect understanding. "Since they're going to gossip, anyway, I suggest we say to hell with it and give them something juicy to gnaw on."

Her chin shot up. "And what would that be, Mr. Sinclair?"

"Well, instead of setting off fireworks the way they expect, we could pretend to be friendly. One of us could even laugh."

His comment caused Elizabeth to do just that. Cutter pulled out a chair and she settled into it. Then she fixed her cool gaze on Nikki, who waited to be cut to shreds in typical sweet-as-honey Southern fashion. Instead, Elizabeth inclined her head. "It's always good to see you, Nikki. Your mother and I had lunch just Wednesday past. I swear she looks younger every time I see her, which leaves me fit to be tied."

"She'll be thrilled to hear it."

"Don't you dare tell her I said that. There'll be no living with her."

The waitress stopped by, her avid gaze passing over the group, no doubt committing any comments she might have caught to memory, as well as everyone's demeanor. "Herbal tea, please, Jo," Elizabeth requested, obviously familiar with their waitress. "And are the blueberries local?"

"Yes, ma'am. We received a delivery just yesterday."

"In that case, bring me one of Maybelle's Bluebelles, otherwise I'll never hear the end of it," she ordered, referring to the pastry that was a house special. "In fact, bring some for the entire table, my treat."

"Yes, Miz Kincaid." Jo's fascinated gaze landed on Jack and clung, before reluctantly switching to Nikki. "And you, ma'am?"

"Coffee, black."

Jack nodded. "The same."

Cutter spoke up for the first time, offering the waitress an easygoing smile. "Make that three." He waited until she'd drifted out of hearing range before adding, "I hope you don't mind that I tagged along. Considering the topic of conversation, I knew this would be difficult for Elizabeth."

"I'm glad you're here," Jack surprised them all by saying before meeting Elizabeth's gaze. "And I apologize for causing you any more stress. I'm sure you're aware that the police investigation has shifted recently and I'm now under suspicion for Reginald's murder."

"I'm aware," she said shortly, "though I'm not sure how that has anything to do with me."

"It doesn't, but I'm hoping if I can gather as many facts about Dad—Reginald's death as possible, I'll be able to clear my name."

His slight stumble over his reference to his father didn't go unnoticed. For an instant, Elizabeth stiffened then she shocked him by offering a quick glance of sympathy. "He was your father, Jack. You won't upset or offend me by calling him that. You have as much claim on the word as any of my children."

For an instant, Jack closed his eyes. He hadn't expected such graciousness from a woman he'd come to realize was the most wronged of any of them. Nor had he expected the wave of shame and contrition that flowed through him. As much as he loved and admired his mother, this was one area and one subject where they differed dramatically.

And maybe it would help to say as much, to show the same graciousness that had been extended to him. "They both wronged you, Elizabeth. For what it's worth, I'm sorry. He should have asked for a divorce before he ever approached my mother again. It's what an honorable man would have done."

Elizabeth's mouth trembled for a brief moment before she steadied it. "You're quite right," she whispered. "It would have been more honorable. Just as it would have been more honorable for me to have asked for that divorce three years ago when I found his will and discovered your existence." Her mouth tightened. "And your mother's. I suppose Reginald and I were both foolishly attempting to protect our children, when in truth they didn't need our protection at all."

Cutter closed his hand over hers and squeezed. "That's all water under the bridge now, Lizzie. Something that can't be changed."

"Still, it hurt to learn he loved another woman more than he ever loved me. Just as it hurt when he left her a letter without offering me so much as a word of explanation."

Jack's eyes narrowed, sharpened. "I must have missed that at the reading of the will. You didn't receive a letter from Dad?"

Four

Pride came to Elizabeth's rescue and her chin shot upward while her green eyes turned vivid with anger. "I did not," she stated crisply. "Even worse were the final words spoken between us. While all of you were left with words of love, I'm left with words of anger. Words neither of us can take back."

"That was the night he was murdered, when you brought his dinner to the office?"

"It was."

The waitress arrived just then, looking distinctly put out when they all fell silent. She unloaded her tray onto their table. After checking to make certain they had everything they needed, she reluctantly departed again.

"Mrs. Kincaid—Elizabeth," Jack corrected himself. "Tell me what happened that night. What did you see? What did Dad say to you?"

She reached for a Bluebelle and broke off a fragment,

though she didn't eat it. Instead, she crumbled the flaky pastry between her fingers. "I've thought about it and thought about it until my head's ready to explode. I exited the elevator and walked to his office. I knocked, waited a bit for him to tell me to come in and then I—"

"Why did you have to wait?" Jack interrupted a recital he could tell had become rote.

Elizabeth hesitated as though no one had ever asked that question before. She brushed a hand through her auburn hair and gave an impatient shrug. "Goodness, Jack. After all these years I know better than to interrupt him when he's on the phone. At least that was my impression." Her brow wrinkled as she sifted through her memories of the event. "Now that I think about it, there was more of a delay than I'd have expected. Then he said to come on in."

"Was he still on the phone?"

"No, he'd already hung up." She gave an elegant wave, dismissing the subject. "Who knows, maybe he was talking to your momma. Anyway, I had his dinner in a large bag—his favorite, roast beef and potatoes. We'd had an argument the night before about how moody he'd been lately."

"Did he explain why he'd been so moody?" Jack interrupted.

Elizabeth shook her head, quite definite. "No, he just said it had to do with a recent problem that had cropped up and that he was afraid he'd delayed too long resolving it."

"What happened when you walked into his office?"

"I asked Reginald something innocuous like how long he thought he'd be, or how business was going. He snapped at me, told me he didn't have time for my fool questions and to get on home." Tears sparkled in

Elizabeth's lovely eyes. "He didn't even want the dinner I'd brought. I ended up throwing it away."

"I'm sure he didn't mean it," Nikki murmured. "He always spoke about you with the utmost respect. Despite everything, I know he cared deeply for you."

She dabbed at her eyes with her napkin. "Thank you, dear. I'd like to believe that, but the evidence suggests otherwise."

"Did he often snap at you like that?" Jack asked.

"Never. Even when we fought, he was never cruel or cutting the way he was this time. I guess that's why I was so hurt. I told him he had no call to speak to me that way and stormed out. I got back on the elevator. It stopped once on its return to the lobby and Brooke joined me. We exchanged a few words, though I was too upset at the time to remember what they were. Then I left the building and drove straight to Cutter's."

"Thank you," Jack said, and meant it.

"You know…" Nikki offered slowly, "I don't remember Charles saying anything about a phone call."

Elizabeth shook her head in confusion. "I'm sorry. Charles…?"

"Charles McDonough, the lead detective in the case."

"Oh, yes, of course." She gave a delicate shiver. "He made my life rather difficult for several months."

Jack could sympathize. Charles had given him some uncomfortable moments, as well. "Elizabeth, did you mention that phone call to Charles?"

She hesitated, taking a moment to consider. "I don't believe I did. To be honest I forgot about it until just now when you asked the question."

"Thank you. You've been quite helpful."

She lifted a shoulder in a dismissive shrug. "If you

say so. I'm not sure I said anything terribly earthshaking."

Jack returned his napkin to the table. They should go now. He should walk away this minute before he said something he'd regret. After all, she was a Kincaid. Though he sympathized with her, that didn't change his overall feelings toward her family or his plans for the annual meeting later this month.

But he found he couldn't just walk away. Maybe it was having Nikki there, her emotions so palpable he could practically touch them. Maybe it was seeing Elizabeth's untempered vulnerability, her pain and grief. Or maybe it was her generous acceptance of him that caused the breach in defenses he's spent a lifetime building. Regardless of the cause, he felt compelled to speak.

"Dad talked to me about you one time," he informed her in a low voice. He forced himself to continue, despite the difficulty of the memory or his reluctance to share it. "I was a teenager, grappling with my confusion over my parents' relationship and not understanding why my father refused to acknowledge me as his son. I called you a rather vile name." He offered a contrite smile. "One you clearly didn't deserve."

"I'm surprised Reginald didn't agree with you," Elizabeth retorted with a hint of acid.

Jack's smile grew. "He knocked me on my ass and dragged me outside for a man-to-man talk."

Elizabeth blinked in surprise. "He did? How…unexpected."

"I think that's what I'm trying to say, Elizabeth," Jack said gently. "It shouldn't be unexpected. That day he told me that he'd been very fortunate to love two of the finest women he'd ever known. He said he married you for money and status, but stayed with you out of love and respect. He described the life you'd carved out together and for the five children you shared. And I could tell you all meant the world to him."

Elizabeth's brows drew together and her eyes darkened in reluctant sympathy. "That must have been very difficult for you to hear."

Beside him, Nikki reached beneath the table and took his hand in hers. He spared her a brief glance, one that told her how much he appreciated her support. God, how he'd wanted to be part of the life his father had described. Had craved it with a yearning so intense it threatened to eat him alive. He wanted to belong the way his father's other children belonged, to have brothers and sisters who loved him and squabbled with him, but who in the end accepted him as one of their own.

That day with his father, he realized it would never happen. That for the rest of his life he'd be an outsider, never acknowledged. Never accepted. Never a Kincaid. It had been one of the worst days of his entire life and no doubt ignited the fire that raged within him to compete. To win. To prove he deserved a place in their lives, even if he had to bully his way in and seize it through sheer force.

But that wasn't the message he wished to convey. Elizabeth needed something far different from him and for some odd reason, he felt compelled to give it to her. "Dad told me that you were one of the most generous women he'd ever met. Just so you know, you share that quality with my mother. But he said you also possessed a sweetness that most women from your world lack. He said I could condemn him all I wanted, that he more than deserved it. But I was never to disrespect my mother or you, for you both acted solely out of love and always put others ahead of your own needs, something he'd never learned to do. I'd have to agree with him, since otherwise, none of us would be in our current situation. And then he said of all those he'd hurt, you were the most innocent and the most wronged. I also have to agree with him about that."

For an instant, Elizabeth stared blindly. Then tears flooded her eyes and she turned into Cutter's waiting embrace. It took her several minutes to recover her composure, but when she did, she revealed the profound sweetness that Reginald had referred to, along with an intense gratitude. "I can't thank you enough, Jack. What you just said… I think that's better than any letter could possibly have been."

He frowned. "I will say it doesn't make sense that he didn't leave you a letter, Elizabeth. Maybe he intended to do it and died before he could complete the task. I'm sure yours would have been the most difficult letter he had to write."

Elizabeth shook her head. "I don't think so. I think yours would have been the most difficult because he knew he'd deprived you of so much. Would you mind my asking what he did say to you?"

Jack hesitated. "I haven't opened it," he admitted. "I've actually been tempted to burn it."

"But you haven't," she observed shrewdly. "I think you just need time and distance before you read it. I suspect you'll know when that moment finally arrives. Until then, don't do anything you may regret. Promise me you won't."

He inclined his head. "Fair enough. Since it's you asking, I can't refuse."

She hesitated. "I assume you received your invitation to Matthew and Susannah's wedding next weekend."

"I did."

"I truly hope you plan to attend." She spared Nikki a quick smile. "Please bring Nikki, if you'd like."

With no other choice but to accept the invitation, he inclined his head. "I'd like that."

The four stood and Jack collected the bill, waving off Cutter's offer to pay. When he held out his hand to Elizabeth, she brushed it aside and gave him a quick, fierce hug instead. He didn't know who she'd surprised more by the impromptu gesture, him or the rest of the coffeehouse patrons. Then she turned and walked away, her head held high, her back ramrod straight. But he couldn't help noticing a spring in her step that had been lacking when she arrived.

He stared after her, broodingly. Damn it, why did she have to hug him? Despite having shared that long-ago memory with her, he'd still managed to hold a piece of himself in reserve. To stay safely behind the walls he'd built and limit the damage their interaction had caused. But that hug had yanked him out into the open. Bared him. Left him more vulnerable than he could ever recall being. And he didn't like it. Not one tiny bit.

The instant they hit the sidewalk, he drew Nikki to one side and retrieved his cell phone. Punching in a number, he waited until the call connected.

"Harold Parsons."

"Harold, Jack Sinclair here."

"You do realize this is Saturday, don't you, boy?" The question escaped in a gruff voice, a perfect match for what Jack recalled of the lawyer's beetled brows, gray tufts of hair and shrewd gaze. "My offices are closed. Call back Monday."

"If you're closed, why did you answer the phone?"

A long, irritated sigh came across the airwaves. "What do you want?"

"My father left letters for everyone as part of his final bequest. But Elizabeth never received one. Why is that?"

"How should I know?" Harold snapped. "It wasn't in the file, therefore there wasn't one."

"Dad wouldn't have slighted her that way," Jack insisted. "When did he write the letters?"

"The last time he updated his will. He always updated the letters at the same time."

"Has there always been one for Elizabeth in the past?"

Harold paused. "Yes…" He drew out the word, his irritation fading as he realized where Jack was going with his line of questioning. "Until this time. Of course, there'd also been one for Alan in the past and there wasn't this time."

"I'm still not buying it, Harold. Alan, okay. He wasn't Reginald's son. But he wouldn't slight Elizabeth that way, nor embarrass her in front of the family. I want you to go through your offices with a fine-tooth comb. He wrote that letter, I'd bet my business on it. If it's gone missing, I want to know when and why. Otherwise, I want it found."

"I'll look into it."

As soon as Jack disconnected the call, Nikki gripped his arm. "What's going on?"

"I think Dad wrote Elizabeth a letter." He shook his head, correcting himself. "I don't think. I know, straight down to my bones, he wrote her one."

"What do you think happened to it?"

"Either the lawyer's office misplaced it. Or it's somewhere in Dad's office."

"If that's the case, maybe we should ask RJ to search Reginald's office."

Jack's mouth twisted in open irony. "Yeah, I'll call him up and suggest he do that. Considering how tight we are after yesterday's confrontation, I'm sure he'll get right on it."

She held his gaze with an uncomfortable steadiness. "If it's for his mother's benefit, he will."

Aw, hell. She was serious. "You really want me to call, don't you?"

"Yes."

"You're not going to let up until I do, are you?"

"Not a chance."

He glared at her, not bothering to disguise his frustration. "You know, today is turning out to be a real pain in the ass. First Elizabeth and now RJ. You do understand that I despise my Kincaid relatives on a good day. When I have to deal with them on one of my few days off, my level of despise increases exponentially."

She patted his arm. "So I gather."

He gave it to her straight. "I'm also trying to destroy them, take over their business and make a misery of their life as they currently know and enjoy it. You get that, don't you?"

"You may have mentioned it a time or two," she conceded with a meekness he didn't buy into for one little minute.

"FYI, helping them out is wreaking havoc on my plans to A) destroy, B) take over, and it sure as hell isn't doing much to C) make a misery of their life as they currently know and enjoy it."

His bitter complaint elicited a sympathetic smile. He didn't buy into that, any more than he bought into her meekness. "Let's help out today. Tomorrow you can get back to putting A through C into motion. You can even add D and E if it makes you feel better."

"Done." He stabbed a finger in her direction. "And just so we're clear, I'm holding you to that. In fact, I might just make you help."

She smiled blandly. "What do you think I've been doing?"

"If that's your idea of help, I'm in serious trouble."

"Nothing." RJ's voice sounded ripe with irritation, an attitude mirrored in his taut, withdrawn stance.

Clearly, he blamed Jack for getting his hopes up, Nikki realized uneasily. Not what she'd anticipated from this latest gathering of brothers.

"Nothing here, either," Matt agreed, also scowling. He shot Jack a look that blistered him for their wasted time and effort. "Not that I expected there to be."

RJ addressed Nikki in a testy voice. "I certainly hope you didn't get Mom's expectations up about this business with the letter."

She offered a reassuring smile. "Your mother has no idea we even suspect there's a letter. It was Jack who figured it out."

"Sinclair?" Both brothers spoke in unison, their gazes swiveling to stare—okay, glare—at Jack.

"What the hell are you up to?" RJ demanded.

"I already explained that to you. Try to keep up, Kincaid," Jack retorted.

To Nikki's concern he sounded tired, even his sarcasm bordering on exhausted. Of course, it had been a rough two days for him and the Kincaids weren't making it easy to drop decades' worth of barriers and give them the opportunity to know the man behind the ruthless facade. How odd that it had never occurred to Jack that instead of always standing on the outside, looking in, all he had to do was open the door to his own life and he'd no longer be on the outside. He wouldn't be alone anymore. He'd have created his own family, his own circle of friends, his own home, full of warmth and love.

This morning had provided an excellent start, thanks to Elizabeth's innate kindness. She had slipped under Jack's guard the easiest, but then, that was her nature. At heart she was a sweet, generous woman who went out of her way to help others. Her sons would be far harder to coax inside. Nikki's chin set into a stubborn line. But she would find a way. While Jack worked his way from A to E, she intended to work her way from one to six, straight through the Kincaid lineup— including Elizabeth—in order to win them all over to Jack's cause. One big, happy family. Or they would be until the annual meeting.

"This has been a colossal waste of time. I'm out of here," RJ announced. He lobbed a final warning shot in Jack's direction on his way out of the door. "Stay out of Kincaid business, Sinclair. You do anything to hurt our mother and I'll bury you so deep they'll need a backhoe to dig out all the broken pieces."

Matt started for the door after his brother then hesitated before leaving the room. "Why do you want that letter, Sinclair?"

"The hell if I know."

Matt turned and faced him, eyeing him closely. "I'm serious. Why?"

Jack was going to lie; Nikki could see it in his expression. She crossed to his side and looked up at him. She could practically feel the waves of pain and resistance pouring off him. Gently, she slid a hand around his waist and pressed close in open support. For a long, tense moment she waited for him to make a decision. Open up or close down. No doubt his instinct screamed for him to lie. To reject the opportunity to reveal the heart of the man lurking behind the merciless business facade. She knew an instant before he spoke that she'd won this round.

"You know our father." Each word escaped as though forced from him. "And you know how he felt about your mother. He'd never have insulted her that way. There's a letter for her somewhere."

Matt's eyebrows shot up in open skepticism. "And you're going to find it?"

"If I can."

"Just because it's the right thing to do?"

"Something like that."

He was closing down again, Nikki could feel it. Maybe he would have if Matt hadn't asked a question that caught Jack completely off guard. "Why did you visit my son in the hospital?"

Matt had faced a parent's worst nightmare when his three-year-old son, Flynn, had developed aplastic anemia following a strong viral infection. Fortunately, the medication the boy received worked its magic. Otherwise, his biological mother, Susannah, would have donated her bone marrow in an attempt to save their son's life. Her advent into their lives had led to a romance between her and Matt, one that promised another Kincaid wedding next week.

"Why did I visit Flynn?" Jack's mouth curved in a sardonic smile. "I don't know, Matt. Because it was the right thing to do?"

"Well, and because he wanted to see if he was a bone marrow match," Nikki added irrepressibly.

Her words couldn't have had a more dramatic impact

if she'd stripped naked and performed a hula dance on Reginald's desktop. Matt's mouth dropped open and he stared in patent disbelief. Slowly he shook his head. "No way."

Jack's smile turned cynical and he shot Nikki a glare that promised future retribution. Well, she could handle it if it meant Matt saw his brother in a slightly different light than he'd been portrayed to date.

"Right," Jack said, his voice desert-dry. "No way I'm capable of something like that."

"You offered to donate bone marrow?" Matt repeated.

"It was an easy offer to make since I doubt I'd have been a match."

Matt's expression grew more intent. "And if you had been?"

Jack shrugged, remaining mute.

Nikki rolled her eyes in exasperation. "Give your brother a little credit, Matt. You don't get tested if you don't intend to go through with the procedure if there's a match."

"He's not my brother," the two brothers said in unison.

A strained silence fell between them for an instant, one Matt finally broke. "When you visited Flynn in the hospital... You said you'd once been hospitalized as a kid. What happened, exactly?" A tautness dropped over his features. "You didn't need a bone marrow transplant, did you?"

Jack shook his head. "Nothing so dramatic."

Nikki shrugged. "If you consider getting hit by a car nothing dramatic. Personally, I find it terrifying."

He turned on her. "Would you cut it out! Stop telling them personal information. It's none of their business."

"Of course it's their business. They're family."

"When...when did that happen?" Matt stumbled over the question. "Were you all right? I mean, obviously you're all right. Hell."

"Awkward, isn't it?" Jack murmured.

Matt shook his head and then started to laugh. "Damn awkward. It shouldn't be. It should all be straightforward. I hate you. You hate me. Everyone's happy." His green eyes showed a hint of the same warmth as his mother's. "So, what happened, Sinclair? Were you so busy trying to take over the world even then that you weren't paying attention to where you were walking?"

To Nikki's profound relief she saw an answering amusement glittering in Jack's blue eyes. "My brother, Alan, was the one not paying attention. My mistake was knocking him out of the way and taking the hit for him. Not that the little brat ever thanked me. Denied he was even there."

"How old were you?"

Jack's smile faded. "Twelve. It was the Fourth of July."

"Oh, my birthday." Matt ran a quick calculation. "I'd have been all of one."

"Yeah, I know."

Matt stiffened, his gaze sharpening. "How hurt were you?"

"I'm still here, aren't I?"

But Matt wasn't buying it. "It was touch-and-go, wasn't it? And I'm willing to bet your mother called our father. Did he show up?"

"Eventually."

"Meaning, no. He didn't come, despite the fact that you might have died. And all because it was my first birthday and my mother would have suspected something if he'd taken off. So, you were on your own."

"Not at all. My mother was there." Jack shrugged. "She's a nurse. Probably saved my life that day since she knew what to do to stop the bleeding."

Matt nodded, a grimness cloaking him. "That's why you visited Flynn. Why you brought a toy. Because you didn't have any aunts or uncles or brothers or sisters to visit you when you were in the hospital."

"I had my mother." Jack repeated then attempted to deflect attention from himself. "Does it matter why, Matt? Whether you like it or not, Flynn's my nephew. He's an innocent and deserved my help regardless of how I might feel about his father."

"Of course, if you hurt Flynn's father, you also hurt Flynn," Nikki inserted smoothly. Based on Jack's reaction, that detail had never occurred to him. Typical. He was so focused on his own goals, he didn't always look at the big picture. Deciding that she'd helped heal as much of the breach between them as she could, she deliberately changed the subject. "Matt, do you know whether the police checked The Kincaid Group phone records the night of your father's murder?"

Instantly, his wariness returned. "Why?"

"Your mother said something about Reginald being on the phone when she arrived with his dinner. I was just curious to know who he might have spoken to."

"Huh." Matt's brows pulled together. "I think you'd have to ask Detective McDonough about that. I'm pretty sure the police obtained a court order requesting them. Since no one mentioned anything more about it, I assume either Dad didn't make or receive any phone calls that night, or they weren't significant to the case."

"Would you be willing to contact Charles and ask for a copy of those phone records?"

His wariness turned to open suspicion. "Why would I do that? And even more importantly, why would Mc-Donough agree?"

She answered his second question first. "He might agree if you explained that you wanted to see if anything jumped out at you. You'd know better than anyone who your father would normally speak to in the course of doing business. Considering the case isn't moving forward very fast, Charles might just agree." She used every ounce of persuasive ability she possessed. "Besides, how can showing us the records hurt anything? Maybe, just maybe it could help."

Matt stewed about it for a moment before reluctantly nodding. "I'll ask, but I make no promises."

The two men stared at each other for a long moment then with a sigh of profound irritation, Jack stuck out his hand. "Thanks."

Matt hesitated, just as his mother had when first offered Jack's hand. Then he took it in a firm grip. "Don't mention it. Apparently, family does this sort of thing. Like bring toys to their nephew in the hospital and have their bone marrow tested."

Jack nodded. "Apparently they do."

"They also attend family weddings. You'll be there next Saturday?"

"Wouldn't miss it for the world."

Jack turned on Nikki the instant they left The Kincaid Group building. "Don't do that again."

She smiled up at him, the very picture of innocence. "Do what?" she asked.

"Nuh-uh. I'm not buying it, sweetcakes. Not the

smile. Not the wide-eyed 'why whatever do you mean, butter wouldn't melt in my mouth' look. None of it."

"Why whatever do you mean?"

He pulled to a halt in the middle of the sidewalk. Sun rained down on them, the air dripping with humidity, while a fresh breeze from off the harbor tumbled her dark hair around a face bright with laughter. The afternoon light caught in her blue eyes so they glittered more brilliantly than the gemstones they resembled. The annoyed words he'd been about to utter died unspoken. All he could do was stare.

He reached for her, lifted her onto her tiptoes and took her mouth in a kiss he meant to be hard and passionate, but ended up landing with a soft, persuasiveness that had her moaning in delight. Her arms encircled his neck and she leaned into him, her feminine curves locking against him, fitting in place so perfectly he couldn't doubt they'd been two parts designed to one day become a whole. If they'd been anywhere other than standing on a sidewalk on Charleston's busy East Battery, he'd have made love to her right then and there.

Instead, a modicum of sanity prevailed and he gave her mouth a final nibbling taste before pulling back. "You have to stop interfering, Nikki. I'm dead serious. Now I'm stuck—correction—*we're* stuck attending another one of their weddings. If I'd wanted a relationship with the Kincaids, I'd have formed one long ago."

To his annoyance, she shook her head, her arms still linked around his neck. "No, you wouldn't have," she argued. "Even though all of you are grown and more than capable of forming your own decisions, you continued to respect your father's wishes by keeping your distance from the Legitimates, as you call them."

"Has it occurred to you I kept my distance because I had no interest in knowing them?"

Her expression grew even more tender. "You may have told yourself that, but it isn't true."

If she weren't still holding him in place, he'd have ended the conversation by simply walking away. And though he could have pulled loose, for some reason he didn't. "You're calling me a liar?" he asked.

"No. I just think when it comes to the Kincaids you've been very careful not to look at your own motivations too closely."

"Nikki, this is a pointless discussion. Now let go of me. I'm tired and I'd like to head home and enjoy just a few minutes of what's left of the day."

But she didn't let go of him. Nor did she stop pushing, pushing, pushing. "Jack, for once in your life, stop. Think. Consider why you've made the choices you have."

His mouth took on a hard, stubborn slant. "If you mean why I'm intent on taking down the Kincaids—"

"No, that's not what I mean. I mean, why did you decide to start up a competing company? Of all the possible businesses and professions you could have gone into, why in the world would you choose the very one where—guaranteed—you were bound to run into your brothers and sisters at some point? Why, Jack?"

This time he did grab her hands and yank them from around his neck. He took a deliberate step backward. Then another, rejecting every aspect of the question. Without a word, he turned and walked away. But no matter how long or how far he walked, he couldn't escape Nikki's question. Nor could he escape the painful knowledge that pierced him like a dagger. On some level Nikki was right. He'd wanted to run into the

Kincaids when he started up Carolina Shipping. He'd wanted them to know he existed. He wanted them to know the truth.

He was their brother.

Five

Nikki finally located Jack two hours later, sitting near the General William Moultrie statue on the outskirts of White Point Gardens, overlooking Charleston Harbor. She thought it appropriate that she found him beside the man responsible for the protection and defense of Charleston during the Revolutionary War since Jack so often assumed that role within his own family.

He didn't look at her when she took a seat on the cement wall beside him. After a few minutes passed, he broke the uneasy silence. "How is it that you see things the way you do?"

"I don't know. I guess it's a gift." She stared out across the water and shrugged. "Or maybe you'd consider it a curse. I just know it's a talent my father had, one he passed onto me. I think it's part of what made him such a great cop. He could talk to someone for a bit and get under their skin. Figure out what motivated them and why. He once told me that figuring out the motivation often helped him solve the case."

"You've gotten under my skin." Now he did look at her, his gaze dark with pain. "And I'm not sure I like it. I'm not sure I want you there."

She bowed her head and nodded. "I understand." She tried not to show the hurt, though she felt it. Dear God, how she felt it. "Maybe that's why so many cops prefer to associate with other cops." Her hand fluttered in a swift, helpless gesture. "Not only do they understand the demands and pressures of the job, but they don't end up feeling what the average person feels—like they're living under a microscope."

"That's not what I meant." He reached for her, tugged her close. "You've never made me feel like I'm living under a microscope. You just…" He released a sigh of sheer frustration. "You see far too much. And for some reason your vision is much clearer than my own."

She snuggled in, her throat constricting, making it difficult to speak. "You're just too close to the problem, that's all. I can see it because I have emotional distance."

Only she didn't. Not when it came to Jack. At some point in the past four months he'd become her world. And she couldn't imagine her life without him in it. She shut her eyes, praying she wouldn't start crying at the bittersweet awareness filling her. Before too much longer, she might not only have to imagine life without him, but live it without him, as well. His hand shifted and he caught her chin, turning her so she was forced to look at him.

"You need to stop now," he told her gently. "You need to understand that I don't have the sort of connection to the Kincaids you're hoping for and I never will. All of your attempts to create that connection are pointless because my plans for them haven't changed and they won't."

"Jack—"

He cut her off without hesitation. "Stop, Nikki. This isn't open for debate or discussion. I'm telling you how it's going to be. You can either continue to be with me… or we end this now. But this desire you seem to have of uniting the two families won't work. Ever. There's too much bad history between us for that to happen."

"There's *no* history between you," Nikki objected heatedly. "There was history between you and your father, and between your parents. But you only met your brothers and sisters five months ago. There's no reason you can't have some sort of positive relationship with them. Look at how well it went today with Elizabeth and Matt." Enthusiasm swept through her words. "Don't you get it? It's entirely up to you. If you'd just drop this vendetta you have going and consider working with them, instead of against them—"

He stopped her using the most effective means at his disposal. He kissed her. Whereas before his kiss had been gently persuasive, this one took command. This one led, giving her the option of following…or withdrawing. But she couldn't withdraw. It was far too late for that. Instead, she surrendered, utterly.

Her head tipped back against his shoulder and she opened to him, accepting his possession, shivering beneath the skillful way he aroused and teased. They were so perfectly mated in all the ways that counted. Their intellect. The love that burgeoned between them, bit by delicious bit. Their sense of humor. Their work ethic. Their generosity and protectiveness toward others. Even the way they viewed the world and those in it—with the single unfortunate exception of the Kincaids. Why couldn't Jack see that?

But he didn't and one look at the hard determination cutting across his face warned that he'd set his plans in stone. Any hope she had of swaying him would not just meet with disappointment, but with disaster.

"I will not tolerate any further interference on your part," he told her, his voice underscoring the hint of mercilessness she'd caught in his expression. "Are we clear on that point, Nikki?"

She pulled back from his embrace. "We're clear. But I don't have to like it." She folded her arms across her chest. "And in case *I* haven't been clear on that point. I don't."

"I believe you've been crystal clear," he said with a slight smile that did nothing to improve her temper. "Are you going home or would you like to spend the night at my place?"

She gave herself permission to stew for a full thirty seconds before lifting her shoulder in a quick, impatient shrug. "Your place."

"Excellent. We can break in the hot tub together."

Her eyes widened. "Hot tub? You have a hot tub? When did you get a hot tub?"

He tucked a lock of hair behind her ear. "It was meant to be a surprise for this weekend. I had it installed yesterday. You have no idea how hard I've worked to resist christening it without you. It's been sitting there calling to me all day."

"Funny." She slanted him a swift look. "I hear it calling to me, too. In fact, I think my name's written all over it with a giant arrow that says, 'plant backside here.'"

"I might have noticed your name." He held up two

fingers pinched together. "In teeny-tiny print and a warning label. Something to do with combustible materials."

She allowed her irritation to fade and amusement to take its place. "Combustible only when combined."

"Oh, I do plan on combining. And shaking. Maybe lighting a fuse or two."

Her mouth curled into a reluctant smile. As much as she wanted to stay angry at him, it wouldn't serve any useful purpose. "I think you already lit a fuse or two." She caught his hand in hers and tugged. "Come on. Let's go watch the fireworks."

"To hell with watching." He scooped her close. "I plan to set them off. Personally."

Nikki stretched out on one of the extra wide lounging platforms of Jack's hot tub and leaned her head back against his shoulder. With the simple push of a button pulsating jets exploded to life, sending warm water bubbling around them. A soft moan escaped her and she followed Jack's example of closing her eyes and allowing the swirling water to sweep away her cares—particularly those about the Kincaids and how she'd execute her plan to unite Jack with his brothers and sisters now that he was on to her.

"I think I just tripped and fell into paradise," she told him.

"Thank you."

Nikki gave a snort of laughter. "Falling onto you is heaven. Falling onto you while in a hot tub is paradise."

"I believe you've overlooked a step."

"What step is that?"

"The one where you're naked when you tripped and fell on me while in a hot tub." He opened a single eye and lifted a questioning eyebrow. "Explain again why you made us wear swimsuits?"

"Oh, I don't know…" A hint of sarcasm competed with laughter. "Maybe the small matter of our sitting on your deck out in the open."

"That's what the privacy screens are for. Besides, there aren't any homes nearby. I bought the property all around this place to ensure my privacy."

"And if someone wanders down the beach?"

"We're too far away for them to see anything… Much." His nimble fingers skated along her spine and an instant later the top of her swimsuit floated away. "There. That's a huge improvement. At least, we're halfway there."

Water frothed around her breasts like a teasing caress. She'd never realized how arousing pulsating water could be. "Would it help move us closer to paradise if I mention that the bottoms tie on?" Nikki tilted her head to glance at him. "No knots, either."

Jack's slow smile had heat gathering low in her belly, sliding like silk into her veins where it throbbed and pulsated in rhythm with the water jets. "So all I have to do is give them a little tug?" His hand brushed the curve of her hip. "Like this?"

A moment later her swimsuit bottoms bobbed to the surface, followed by a pair of male trunks. Nikki rolled onto her side to face Jack, supported by the churning water. Since their return to his beach house he'd relaxed. Well, as much as he ever relaxed. She'd pushed too hard, too soon. She realized that now.

Maybe if the annual shareholders meeting wasn't taking place so soon, a meeting in which a new president and CEO would be voted in to replace the late Reginald Kincaid, she wouldn't have had to escalate her plan to unite Jack with the Kincaids. Clearly, reconciling with two Kincaids in one day had been more than Jack could handle. That, combined with her assessment of the career he'd pursued and his motivation for choosing that career, had thrown him into full emotional retreat.

She slid her fingertips along his stubbled jawline then followed the contours of his mouth, gathering his smile in the palm of her hand, as well as a lingering kiss. "What are you in the mood to eat for dinner tonight?" she asked.

"You. Just you."

She laughed, delighted they'd gotten back onto more familiar footing. "No doubt you'd find that tasty, but not very filling."

"We can place an order at Indigo's if seafood appeals. I know how much you like that place."

"They deliver?" she asked in surprise.

His smile turned smug. "They will for me." His hand cupped her bottom and he urged her closer. "But later. Much later."

Jack's body slid across Nikki's and she shuddered beneath the abrasive combination of the foaming water and the light pelt of hair covering his chest and legs. Her nipples tightened, peeking above the surface like a pair of dusky pearls. He lowered his head and caught first one then the next between his teeth and she groaned, sliding her fingers into his hair and anchoring him at her breast.

And all the while his nimble fingers played beneath the surface, as tantalizing as the churning jets at stoking the heat gathering there. Her legs parted and her hips tilted upward, offering herself to him. Instead of mating their two bodies, he continued to tease, easing a finger into her warmth, sending her desire skyrocketing to an even higher level.

"I think I see fireworks," she said with a helpless groan.

"I haven't heard them go off, yet."

She couldn't stand another minute and she reached for him, fisting his hard length in her hands and fitting him to her. He sank inward and she shuddered. It took a few tries before they found their rhythm, the water throwing them off. And then the fire caught: a screaming flash that burned an unstoppable path from one to the other. His name escaped in a powerful rush, bursting into the air. Jack surged into her and Nikki arced helplessly upward, exploding into the grand finale.

They lingered there, the brilliance dazzling in its aftermath. Then bit by bit they drifted back to earth, sinking into the comforting embrace of the warm water, dissolving against each other in a tangle of arms and legs, lingering kisses and soothing strokes. Nikki closed her eyes and burrowed close, more vulnerable than she could ever remember feeling.

When would it fade? When would this desperate need for him ease into something more manageable, something that didn't threaten to break her heart? Maybe it never would. Their relationship hung by a thread, dangling above a bottomless chasm. The instant Jack discovered she owned the controlling ten percent shares of Kincaid stock—that she could throw control of The Kincaid Group into either his lap or RJ's, that thread would snap. Because she knew Reginald had intended the position of president and CEO to fall to RJ, had been told so by the late patriarch, himself. And no matter how much she loved Jack, she couldn't—and wouldn't—go against her conscience.

A conscience that demanded she vote for RJ to succeed his father.

Monday came all too soon as far as Jack was concerned. Reluctantly, he and Nikki prepared for work. Over the course of the past several months her business suits had joined his in the closet at his beach house. It never failed to amuse him how she would hang them so they marched boy/girl, boy/girl across the wooden support bar.

By the time he reached the kitchen, Nikki already had the coffee brewing. Though he'd told her repeatedly she didn't need to fix him breakfast, she'd shrugged him off, seeming to enjoy throwing their meal together most mornings. He decided it was a woman thing and let her have her head.

"Veggie omelets?" she offered.

"Sounds great."

It was his usual response since he saw no point in being particular in the face of Nikki's generosity. Then again, maybe tomorrow he'd tease her by saying no just to see what she'd do. A moment's reflection changed his mind. Or maybe he wouldn't. Considering the tension between them over the Kincaid situation, they sure didn't need him adding more conflict to the mix, not over his weak attempt at a joke.

Despite the fact he considered Nikki in the wrong for her interference, he knew she meant well. It was that soft heart of hers getting in the way. Fortunately, he'd put an end to it without too much trouble. And even if he'd been forced to reveal far more personal information to Elizabeth and Matt Kincaid than he would have under normal circumstances, he could live with it, so long as he didn't have to reveal anything further.

Jack pulled the ingredients needed for the omelets from the refrigerator and made short work of chopping the onions and mushrooms, and shredding the spinach. All the while, morning sunshine spilled across the kitchen and landed on Nikki, spotlighting her. It proved a constant distraction. He doubted he'd ever tire of watching her. There was something so vital about her, her movements clean and smooth, yet energetic. Her expression intent, yet easy, with a constant smile half formed on her mouth.

He thought again of the ring he'd bought last month and currently kept tucked away in his dresser drawer. He'd been on the verge of proposing at least a dozen times in the past few weeks. If it hadn't been for his recent discovery that she worked for the Kincaids, he might have already asked. But something held him back. Unfortunately, he knew what it was.

Nikki was keeping another secret.

The realization had come to him over the course of the weekend, beginning with her blatant attempts to resolve the conflict between him and his Kincaid relatives. Her determination had been underscored by something that felt almost like desperation, as though some crucial factor teetered on the outcome of her efforts. His suspicions had solidified during the night when he'd waken to find her standing on the deck, encased in moonlight, her head bent, her shoulders rounded. It was as though she carried an impossible weight. What he hadn't quite figured out yet, was whether or not it had anything to do with the Kincaids, or with her latest campaign of trying to form a connection between him and the Legitimates.

Well, hell. Why not just ask her?

Before he could the doorbell rang. Nikki glanced over her shoulder at him. "Who in the world would visit at this hour?" she asked, her eyebrows drawing together.

"Only one way to find out."

"If it's someone we know, invite them back for omelets," she called to Jack as he left the kitchen. "It won't take me a second to throw together an extra."

He opened the door, unpleasantly surprised to discover the detective assigned to his father's murder investigation standing on his doorstep. Though a couple of inches shorter and a decade or so older than Jack, Charles McDonough was a powerful, impeccably dressed black man with a shaved head that gleamed in the morning light, and dark, patient eyes reflecting a calm intelligence, coupled with an unswerving determination. He'd demonstrated that determination and intelligence the few times he'd interviewed Jack.

Charles inclined his head in greeting. "Good morning, Mr. Sinclair. I'm glad I was able to catch you before you left for the office." He glanced around. "Nice place you have here."

"Thanks." Jack fell back a step. "Come on in."

The detective stepped across the threshold, his deceptively casual gaze taking in every detail of the airy foyer and the magnificent great room that swept toward the back of the house where a wall of sparkling windows overlooked the restless ocean.

"*Very* nice," Charles amended his earlier comment. "If I owned a place like this I'd have every relative in the family tree crawling out for a visit. How about you?"

"I don't have much in the way of family. Just my

brother, Alan, and my mother. But they do stay here whenever they come to Charleston."

The detective gave a brief laugh. "Bet that's more often than you'd like."

"There are times…" Like when Alan arrived on his doorstep unannounced and lingered far longer than the "fish" rule that warned that after three days fish and guests began to smell—and should both be tossed out. Jack gestured toward the hallway to the right. "We're just having breakfast. I've been told to invite you to join us."

"Us?" McDonough's stride checked ever so slightly. "Sorry. It didn't occur to me you'd have company."

"That's all right. I believe you and Nikki are old friends."

"Nikki? Nikki *Thomas?*"

The detective stepped into the kitchen and his face tightened when he caught sight of her. A hint of anger sparked in his dark eyes at the familiar way she moved around the kitchen, her comfortable attitude telling the detective—or maybe screaming at him—she'd been here often enough to make herself at home. Combine that with the early-morning hour and it wasn't hard for a man whose profession made him particularly astute at putting two and two together to do some quick math and come up with a very awkward four…that Jack and Nikki were sleeping together.

Considering Charles and Peter Thomas, Nikki's late father, had once been partners, Jack suspected the detective possessed strong paternal feelings toward her. Paternal feelings that did not bode well for the man who was the "two" having sex with the other "two" in his equation.

Jack sighed. He was so screwed.

Nikki threw a sunny smile over her shoulder. "Morning, Charles."

"What the hell are you doing here, girl?"

"Having breakfast," she replied easily. "When I heard your voice I threw an extra omelet on for you."

"I don't want an omelet."

"Too bad. It's already cooking. I know you, Charles. If you're out and about this early you left before Raye even climbed out of bed. That means you grabbed a cup of coffee and a piece of toast, if that." She waved a hand toward the kitchen table. "Go on and sit. Jack, pour Charles a cup of coffee. He likes it with cream and extra sugar. Raye doesn't let him have the extra sugar, but we'll keep it our little secret."

"Darn it, Nikki," Charles snapped. "You haven't answered my question."

But Jack noticed he took a seat, anyway. Unfortunately the look the detective shot in his direction was just shy of murderous. Better to give him the information up-front and be done with it. "We met shortly after my father's death. We've been dating more than three months. It's serious. You can try to warn her off, but it won't work. She's intent on proving my innocence. Two teaspoons of sugar or three?"

The detective's jaw worked for an endless minute. "Four."

Jack's brows shot upward. "Ouch."

"Yeah, that's what Raye says. Dump it in there, hand it over and keep your comments to your own damn self."

Jack complied before taking a seat across from the detective. Nikki dropped plates in front of the two men and, gazes locked and loaded, they dug in. Charles paused long enough to groan. "God, Nikki, when did you learn to cook this good? You've been taking lessons from your grandma Thomas, haven't you?"

"She might have taught me a couple tricks."

He worked his way through the omelet, scraped his plate clean enough to remove the pattern then shoved it aside. "Knowing you have your nose stuck in this is a royal pain in the ass, Nikki, but it sure explains a thing or two." He eased back in his seat, turning his coffee mug in a slow circle that Jack suspected was his typical thinking mode. "Like why Jack here asked Matt Kincaid to get his hands on The Kincaid Group phone records."

Jack saw red. "Son of a—"

Charles waved him silent. "Kincaid can't lie worth a damn. As soon as I asked him why he wanted a copy he started squirming like a six year-old with both hands and a foot caught in the cookie jar. Didn't take much pushing to find out you were behind it." His gaze switched to Nikki and cooled. "Or rather, Nikki. Her mind works just like her daddy's did."

Nikki's eyes grew misty. "That's the sweetest thing you ever said to me, Charles."

"Why do you want the phone records, girl?"

"Actually, it was Jack's stroke of brilliance."

"Oh, yeah?" The detective's attention returned to Jack and cooled further still. "Exactly what stroke of brilliance might that be?"

Jack debated how much to say, well aware if he didn't explain it to the detective, Nikki would. Since that didn't leave him much choice, he went ahead and laid out his thought process. "The night Dad was killed, when Elizabeth Kincaid brought him his dinner, did she happen to mention to you that she thought she heard Reginald on the phone when she arrived?"

Charles shook his head. "She did not," he stated crisply, clearly displeased he lacked information Jack possessed. "Maybe because he wasn't on the phone. I checked the company phone logs, personally, as well as his cell phone records. One call, outgoing, well before Mrs. Kincaid arrived on the scene. It was to a golfing buddy, confirming a tee-off time."

"Then who was he speaking to?" Nikki asked.

Charles shrugged. "Himself? I've been known to do that when trying to puzzle through a snag in a case. Your daddy used to do it, too," he informed her.

A sudden idea hit Jack, one that explained a lot. "What if…" He spared a quick look in Nikki's direction, who gave him an encouraging nod in return. "What if the killer was in Dad's office when Elizabeth arrived?"

Nikki stared at him in open admiration. "Jack, that's brilliant. That never would have occurred to me, but it sure explains a few things that don't add up."

The detective blinked in surprise. "How did you come up with that idea?"

He didn't use the words "cockamamie idea" but Jack caught the silent inference, nonetheless. He shoved back his chair and stood, pacing toward the bow window overlooking the water, then back again while he gathered his thoughts. "Elizabeth told us that Dad was unusually curt with her. She used the word cruel."

"Yes, she used that word with me, too. Your point?"

"That's not typical of my father. And it sure isn't the way he taught me to treat women. Despite the fact he was involved with my mother, he loved his wife and had the utmost respect for her. When I asked Elizabeth if he'd ever spoken to her like that before, she said he hadn't."

"No, that's what his family and staffed claimed, as

well. It was one of the reasons I doubted her story," Charles agreed. "Go on."

"Why would he act so out of character that night? It doesn't make sense, unless…" He could only hope his idea didn't sound crazy to a trained detective. "Unless the killer was in the room at the time and Dad was trying to protect Elizabeth by getting her out of there in the most efficient and expedient way possible."

"That sounds exactly like something Reginald would do," Nikki murmured. She crossed to Jack's side and gave his hand a swift squeeze. She looked at him, her lovely blue eyes filled with sympathetic understanding. "It would explain so much, wouldn't it? And yet, how sad that one of his last acts was to treat his wife with such cruelty in order to protect her. It probably saved her life, but still… Reginald would have hated having those the final words ever spoken between them."

"Assuming that's what happened," Charles cut in. He tilted his head to one side and closed his eyes as though rolling the thought around, looking for flaws or other possibilities. "That's certainly one plausible explanation. Unfortunately, it's just as plausible that he found out about her affair with Cutter Reynolds and was struggling to come to terms with it. Maybe she arrived before he could regain control of his temper."

"How would he have found out?" Nikki asked. "If he'd hired a private investigator, you would have uncovered that information by now. I mean, none of his children knew. I assume, based on your interviews of friends and business associates, no one else did, either, or they'd have mentioned it."

"And if a friend or business associate knew, I guarantee the rest of Charleston would have heard about it within hours," Jack added a trifle sourly. "Maybe within minutes considering how fast the news spread about Dad's affair with my mother and the fact that I was a product of that affair."

Charles shook his head. "No one mentioned Elizabeth's involvement with Cutter. No one even hinted at the possibility. In fact, after she admitted to the affair, I took another run at those who'd most likely have known. She managed to keep her liaison with Cutter Reynolds well off the radar," he confirmed.

"Then how would Reginald have known?" Nikki asked.

"Okay, let's say that Jack's right and the killer was in the room at the time. So what? What more does that give us than we already know? If we look at what I've learned since Kincaid's murder, certain facts aren't in dispute." He ticked off on his fingers. "Point one. The murderer gained entry to the building through the front door when he walked in with Brooke Nichols shortly before TKG closed for the day. Point two. The killer had to be someone familiar with the building, as well as the location of your father's office, since he didn't ask for directions, but acted as though he knew where he was going. Even more, that he belonged there since it didn't occur to Brooke to question him when he bypassed the check-in desk. Point three. His familiarity with the building and the location of Reginald's office suggests to me that in all likelihood Reginald knew the identity of his murderer. That's why I've been focused on family and close friends. There's only one big stumbling block."

"Everyone has alibis," Nikki said.

"Yes."

Her expression turned uneasy. "Then point four

would be to look at whoever gains the most from Reginald's murder. In other words, motivation."

Charles nodded. "Exactly. So far, the only ones who benefit are the immediate family." The detective's gaze landed long and hard on Jack. "And of all the family you, Sinclair, with your forty-five percent share in TKG stock, stand to gain the most."

Jack forced himself to remain cool and calm, though McDonough ought to have his tough, gotcha look patented. It was that effective. "That doesn't change the fact that I didn't kill my own father. I wouldn't. Damn it, Detective, I couldn't."

"Then why was your car at a parking lot near TKG during the time of the murder?"

"I wish I knew." Since McDonough was being reasonably forthcoming, Jack risked a question. "How is it possible that you have photos or video of my car, but not of me?"

The detective rocked his chair back onto two legs. "That's just it, Sinclair. We do. We have a lovely piece of video featuring you climbing out of your expensive ruby-red Aston Martin and heading off in the direction of TKG."

Six

The words shocked the hell out of Jack and he sank into his chair. *"What?"* He stared at the detective in utter disbelief. He struggled to marshal his thoughts, to make sense out of something so beyond the realm of possibility. "How can you have a video of me when I was never there? It has to be a forgery. I don't know how or why someone would go to such extremes, but I'm telling you, I was working that night. I never left my office until well after the time of Dad's death."

Nikki chimed in, leaping to his defense. "And if it's true, why hasn't he been arrested and thrown in jail?"

Charles ignored her, keeping his gaze fixed on Jack for what seemed like an endless time. Then he closed his eyes and shook his head, swearing under his breath. "You really don't know, do you? Either that, or you're a damn fine actor."

The hot ball of tension forming at the pit of Jack's

stomach eased a fraction. Had the detective been lying in order to gauge his reaction? "All I know is that there's no way you have a video of me at that time and place because I wasn't there," he stated simply.

To his surprise, the detective opened up. "It was raining that night. Pouring. The person who got out of your car is about your size and height and wore a felt hat. You know, like one of those Indiana Jones knockoffs?"

"Right. We had a name for the idiots who wore those."

"Yeah, we did, too." McDonough's gaze flashed with humor and the men had a moment of perfect accord. "Not a word I choose to repeat in front of Nikki," he added.

"So, you never saw his face?" Jack asked.

"No. And what little we could see he disguised with a beard and thick glasses. He also wore a heavy raincoat, which made it even more difficult to get a good feel for his overall build."

Jack mulled over the description. "Any chance it was a woman?"

McDonough shrugged. "Doubtful. According to Brooke Nichols he was tall, nearly RJ's height."

"Another point against me."

"Put together, it makes for some serious circumstantial evidence against you." An uncomfortable silence descended, one McDonough eventually broke. "What did you and your father discuss when you spoke to him the day he died?"

"We spoke the day before, not the day of," Jack said absently.

The detective's gaze sharpened. "Wrong, son. When Matt asked about the phone records, I took another look.

There was a call from Carolina Shipping to your father's private line about an hour before closing."

It took Jack a second to absorb the information. "From Carolina Shipping? The main number or my own private line?"

Charles reeled off the number from memory.

"That's the main line. I always call him from my cell phone or my office, which is a different number from the main line."

"This time you didn't."

Jack's back teeth clamped together. "Why are you so determined to hang me for my father's murder?"

McDonough shrugged. "Why does every new piece of information lead right back to you, Sinclair? It stirs my curiosity, son. It truly does."

"Take another look at those phone records," Jack demanded. "You'll see that every call I ever placed to my father was either from my cell or my personal business line to either his cell or his private office number."

"Then if you didn't call him, who did?"

Jack's expression fell into grim lines. "Good question, one I intend to look into as soon as I get to the office."

"Uh-huh. Well, while you're at it see if you can't come up with an explanation for your car being at the parking lot near TKG. A better one than 'I didn't do it.'"

Jack struggled to contain his frustration. "I have a suggestion. Why don't you show me the video you have?"

Suspicion leaped into the detective's face. "Why?"

"I want to see proof that it's my car."

"They're your tags, son." Even so, McDonough weighed the idea then shrugged. "Set up an appointment and I'll see if I can get it approved." He shoved back his chair and stood. "Nikki, I'd like to warn you off this guy, but I doubt you'll listen."

She offered Charles a gentle smile. "Sorry. I'm in it for the long haul."

He sighed. "I was afraid you'd say that." He nailed Jack with an arctic look. "Walk me out." It wasn't a request.

McDonough didn't speak until they reached the front door. Once there, he turned on Jack, his expression vicious with intent, his voice a dark whisper. "Her daddy and I go way back, Sinclair. He took a bullet meant for me and there's not a day that goes by that I don't live with those consequences."

"She doesn't blame you." It was all Jack could think to say.

"God knows why. That doesn't change the fact that there's not a man on the force who won't stand for her. You understand what I'm saying?" The detective didn't wait for a response. He simply leaned in to hammer home his point. "You hurt her and you won't be able to cross the street without getting arrested for jaywalking. That's assuming you still have a pair of legs capable of walking once we're done with you."

And with that, he spun on his heel and left.

"How bad was the threat?" Nikki asked sympathetically.

Jack spared her a brief glance before returning his gaze to the road. "Nothing I can't handle."

"He didn't mean it."

"Right." A humorless smile cut across his face. "I think you have a tendency to underestimate how protective Charles is of you…and the extent to which he and his cop buddies will go, if our relationship causes you any grief."

"Here's a thought...." she offered brightly. "Don't cause me any grief."

"An excellent plan." His irritation faded, replaced by a sincerity that caused her heart to lurch. "Trust me, the last thing I ever want to do is cause you grief."

"Oh, Jack," she murmured. "There are times you say the most unexpected—and delightful—things."

"I mean them."

"I know you do." She touched his thigh, feeling the muscle clench beneath her gentle caress. "That's what makes them all the more special."

They turned onto East Battery, the traffic thickening. "Your place or mine tonight?" he asked.

"Your place is fine. I want to give that hot tub another spin."

"I'm all over that suggestion." He flashed her a quick grin. "And I hope, all over you."

"Count on it." Reluctantly, she switched her attention to the business of the day. "I assume you're going to look into who might have called your father from Carolina Shipping?"

"It's the first item on my agenda."

"And then?"

"If they made the call from Carolina Shipping, chances are I know the person. So, then I plan to have a long talk with the individual before turning them in to the police. It might be interesting to know their movements the night of my father's murder...including whether there's any chance they had access to my car."

"Huh. Your day sounds a lot more interesting than mine," Nikki complained. "I don't suppose you'd let me tag along for a little while? Two eyes and ears are always better than one."

"What about work?"

"I am working. I'm spying on you, remember?"

To her profound relief, he laughed. "Right, right. Can't imagine how I forgot." Jack passed the access road leading to The Kincaid Group, and continued on. "You can hang with me until lunch. I have meetings this afternoon that I'd rather not postpone."

She started to ask about them, but realizing it might be a conflict of interest, fell silent. They entered the parking lot for Carolina Shipping. Jack pulled into his usual spot beside a hedge of English boxwood, the fragrant scent filling the air. They exited the car and he unlocked the door leading directly from the parking lot into his office, confirming her suspicions about the private entrance. No wonder Charles still considered Jack a viable suspect.

"Too many people were in and out of my office," he said, clearly reading her mind. "Slipping out would have been a foolish chance to take. Anyone could have discovered me gone, and later told the police."

Nikki followed him inside and considered the timeline. "I agree. That's why none of this makes sense."

"So, why am I still a suspect?"

"I don't know, Jack. The killer needed a lot of time, time you didn't have. Not only did he have to wait for the building to clear out to confront Reginald in private, he also had to wait outside TKG so he could walk in with an employee in order to avoid signing the logbook at the front desk."

"That doesn't make sense. If he didn't sign in, why take the log sheet?" Jack asked.

"I wondered about that, too." Nikki worked through

the possibilities. "Maybe in case security made a note of his arrival?"

"Better safe than sorry?"

"It could be just that simple."

He mulled it over and nodded in agreement. "Sounds reasonable." He waved her toward a chair and picked up the phone on his desk and pushed a button. "I'm here, Gail," he informed his assistant. "Would you please have Lynn come to my office when she gets a chance? Thanks." He returned to the timeline. "So, once he's in he'd head for Reginald's office. No point in wasting time, right?"

"Not if he was worried about getting your car back to you before anyone realized it was missing."

"Next problem… How would he know my father would be there, and more importantly, be alone?"

"It was closing time," Nikki said slowly. "Your father often worked late. Let's assume the killer confirmed Reginald was still at the office by calling him from Carolina Shipping. Maybe the killer assumed Reginald would be alone."

"Hmm. Working late seems to run in the family." Jack approached, his gaze warming. "Not as much as it used to. At least, not for the past three months. You've had a seriously negative impact on my workaholic tendencies."

She grinned. "So my diabolical plan is working."

"All too well." He slid his arms around her and nuzzled the sensitive area just beneath her ear, driving every coherent thought from her head. "When I weigh the pleasure of work versus the pleasure of spending those hours with you, work can't compare."

"Oh, Jack," she whispered.

Unable to resist, she kissed him, putting her heart

and soul into the melding of lips and bodies. She'd never known a man capable of arousing her to such extremes, with no more than a lingering glance, a glancing touch, a touching comment. He loosened the buttons of her jacket and slipped his hands beneath, caressing her through the silk shell she wore.

Time drifted away, and she submerged herself in a desire more profound than anything she'd experienced before. Over the past three months she'd done more than fall in love with Jack Sinclair. She'd committed to him, allowed herself to bond with him, to open her emotions so completely that she couldn't imagine being with another man. Ever.

"Nikki, there's something I've been meaning to ask—"

A light tapping on the door interrupted them and the two reluctantly pulled apart. While Nikki buttoned her jacket, Jack made a visible effort to switch gears. Was it wrong she experienced a quick feminine satisfaction that it took several long seconds for him to pull it off?

"Come in," he called out as soon as they were presentable again.

Lynn stepped into the office. "You asked to see me, Jack?" Her gaze landed on Nikki and she smiled with the sort of sweetness Nikki was beginning to associate with her overall personality. "How lovely to see you again, Ms. Thomas. I hope you had a good weekend."

"Excellent, thank you. And please, call me Nikki."

Jack waited through the social chitchat with barely concealed impatience before smoothly switching to the matter at hand. "Lynn, I need to find out who placed a call to my father's office the day of his murder. It would have been from the main company line versus from my office. Around four, I believe. Could you check around?"

A swift frown replaced her sunny smile. "I'll get right on it," she said.

The instant she left, Jack glanced at Nikki. She could see him debating whether to pick up where they'd left off and take her in his arms. With a smile of regret, he stood and wandered over to the coffeemaker he kept by his wet bar. Gail had already brewed the first pot and he poured two cups, handing one to Nikki. He eased his hip onto the corner of his desk and took a slow, appreciative sip. She joined him, sitting in the chair closest to where he lounged and crossed her legs, balancing the cup and saucer on her knee with practiced ease.

"You know, the facts seem fairly straightforward and highly time consuming," Jack said after a moment's thought. "The killer parked in the lot where he was caught on tape. He then proceeded to TKG where he waited outside until he could enter with Brooke. He bypassed the security desk, no doubt taking the stairs to the fourth floor in order to hide until my father was alone, then confronted him."

"He couldn't anticipate Elizabeth arriving with dinner."

Pain touched Jack's face as they moved closer to the point where Reginald had been murdered. "Assuming my father knew his killer—or even if he didn't—there was undoubtedly some discussion both before Elizabeth's arrival and after her departure." His voice deepened. Roughened. "The killer would have had to wait until he was certain Elizabeth was gone and wouldn't hear the gunshot."

Nikki stood and set her coffee aside before doing the same with his. Then she wrapped her arms around him. "Don't. Don't go there," she whispered. "There's no point and your father wouldn't have wanted you to imagine those final moments, but to remember your actual relationship."

He leaned into her, his breathing deep and labored. "God, Nikki. I can't help thinking about how he must have felt during those last seconds of life. Was there something he could have said to prevent it from happening? Something he could have done? Something any of us could have said or done if only we'd known?"

"We may never know." A hint of steel slipped into her voice. "But we can and will figure out who did this. We'll have to be satisfied with that."

He straightened, steel filtering through his own voice, as well. "You're absolutely right. He then shoots my dad and returns to the lobby." The words sounded calm and objective, but she felt the waves of fury and grief rippling beneath.

She clung to her focus, forcing herself to remain logical, aware it was the best way she could help Jack regain his balance and some shred of objectivity. "Okay, but it's after closing and most everyone's gone. I was in the meeting when Tony Ramos, the investigator RJ hired to look into your father's murder, ran through the timeline from that point forward. Jimmy was the security guard on duty that night. He only leaves his station to use the bathroom, and he always locks the front door when the desk is unattended. That means the killer had to wait for Jimmy to take a bathroom break before stealing the page out of the logbook and escaping out the front."

"Did the investigator indicate when that happened?"

Nikki struggled to recall details from a meeting that had taken place over two months earlier. "Jimmy left his post shortly after Brooke and Elizabeth exited the building. He locked the door beforehand, which is his protocol. But when he returned to his station a few minutes later, he found the front door unlocked."

Jack shook his head. "None of this makes sense. I could have discovered my car was missing at any point and notified the cops. Or Reginald's body could have been found and the cops called. That's an endless amount of time. Far too long for me to be a serious suspect."

"Unless they believe you were working in concert with the actual murderer," Nikki suggested reluctantly.

To her surprise, Jack nodded in agreement, taking her comment in stride. "I've begun to suspect the same thing. If you look at the murder from a cop's perspective, it would explain how and why the killer used my car. And why Charles still considers me a suspect." His mouth settled into grim lines. "Whoever took my car was setting me up."

While she'd been avoiding going there, Jack cut straight through to the heart of the matter. "The killer wanted the police to discover the video from the parking lot showing your car—a ruby-red Aston Martin that everyone in Charleston knows you drive," Nikki commented. "Though if you were in cahoots with him it would have been damn stupid of you to have him use such a distinctive vehicle, one that would ultimately lead right back to you."

"And I'm not damn stupid."

"No, you're not." She retrieved her coffee and took a sip, turning various possibilities over in her head. "You know… Maybe we're looking at this backward, Jack. And maybe the police are, too."

He slowly nodded, quick to catch on. "Instead of asking who had a grudge against Reginald and killed him because of it, we should be asking who has a grudge against me and murdered my father, leaving me to take the fall. Unfortunately, there are more than a couple of names on that list, most of which are Kincaids."

A shiver of dread raced through Nikki and her coffee cup chattered against the saucer. "Oh, Jack. What if the police decide you're innocent? I don't think that's going to make the actual murderer very happy. He might decide to come after you, directly. You could be in real danger."

"Don't worry, Nikki. I can look after myself."

He didn't realize it, but his calm reply only increased her fear. How many times had her father said that to her? How many times had he smiled reassuringly—just like Jack was—and told her he'd be fine. That he was a cop, more than capable of looking after himself. It hadn't saved him from a bullet, any more than Reginald had been able to save himself.

Any more than Jack could.

"You can't look after yourself," she retorted sharply, setting her coffee aside. "Not if someone's intent on taking you out. There are too many possible ways to do it. It's too easy to accomplish—just look at what happened to your father."

"And your father?" he asked gently.

Despite the fact that she'd been thinking just that, she shocked them both by bursting into tears. Instantly, he stood and swept her into his arms, holding her close. "Easy, sweetheart, easy. We're going to get this figured out and then we're going to turn the whole problem over to Charles. Whoever killed Dad can't get at me if he's behind bars."

"And if we don't figure out who it is? Or if there's

no proof and the police can't lock him up? Or worse…" She caught her bottom lip between her teeth. "What if the killer implicates you and the police believe him?"

"We deal with one problem at a time. First, we need to figure out who killed Dad. Then we figure out how to prove his guilt while establishing my innocence."

Before she could argue the matter any further, a knock sounded on the door again. Deliberately, Nikki eased from Jack's embrace and pretended to busy herself refilling their coffee cups while she surreptitiously dabbed the tears from her cheeks. Lynn entered the room a moment later. From the corner of her eyes, Nikki saw the receptionist twist her hands together, her agitation palpable.

"Mr. Sinclair?" Her formal address warned her the news wasn't good.

"What did you discover, Lynn?"

"I'm so sorry," she said quickly. "It's all my fault. I let him use the phone. I didn't realize it was the wrong thing to do. If you want my resignation, I'll understand."

"Slow down," Jack said, keeping his voice low and soothing. He took the receptionist's arm and guided her to the couch. "Come and sit. Let's start over. You checked with the other employees about who might have called over to TKG, and…?"

She sank into the thick cushion and regarded him with nervous dread. "And no one had. Then I remembered your brother, Alan, dropped by. He asked to see you, but you'd made it clear you didn't want any interruptions. I explained that to him. He smiled the way he does. He's such a sweetie, you know? Always so accommodating."

"Yeah, that's Alan. Accommodating."

"And he asked if I'd mind if he used the phone. Of course I didn't. I offered mine, but he needed privacy, so I showed him into the conference room. He was only in there about five or ten minutes, though at one point I thought I heard his voice raised. I kind of shrugged it off since maybe he was just joking around with someone. Then he returned. I said goodbye, but he must not have heard me. He just went directly out. Only…"

"It's okay, Lynn. Nothing you say about Alan will upset me."

"He seemed a little angry," she said reluctantly. "Usually he's so easygoing, you know? But I had the feeling that something about that phone call didn't go well and I remember thinking that maybe he hadn't been joking around, after all. Maybe he'd been mad at the person."

"That's great, Lynn, exactly what I needed to know."

"Really?" Her gaze clung to him. "You're not just saying that? I didn't do anything wrong?"

"Really. You didn't do a thing wrong. You can go back to work now."

She beamed, her brown eyes sunny with relief. "Thanks, Jack."

The door closed behind her and Jack looked at Nikki, his eyes glacial.

"Alan?" she asked. "Is it possible?"

"I find it hard to believe my brother would kill Dad." He stood and she didn't think she'd ever seen him appear more intimidating and ruthless. "Even so, I think it's time we paid my little brother a visit."

Seven

The drive to Greenville where Alan and Jack's mother, Angela, lived took just over three hours. Shortly after noon they pulled into the circular driveway of the large mountain estate his father had purchased for his mother. He, Alan and his mother had lived here from the time he'd been ten until he'd gone off to college.

Jack sat in the car and stared at the place he'd once called home. He'd moved out the day he'd graduated, his business degree clutched firmly in hand. He'd never returned, at least not to live. In part it had been to keep the peace with Alan, who'd made it clear Jack wasn't wanted. But mainly he'd been determined to strike out on his own, preferring to earn enough to buy his own home rather than living off the largesse of his father, just as he'd been determined to pay his own way through college. It had been a point of honor and pride.

"Mom broached the possibility of selling the place a

couple of months ago," he informed Nikki. "But Alan became so enraged, she dropped the idea."

"Are they home?" she asked.

"Mom will be at work unless today's a half shift. If that's the case, she'll be home soon. As for Alan..." His mouth curved into a sardonic smile. "Nothing has changed since you were last here. My brother is still between jobs, so he should be around."

"Got it."

Jack didn't bother knocking, but used his key. At the sound of the door opening, Alan appeared in the archway separating the spacious foyer from the living room. An inch or so shy of Jack's six-foot-one height, he had golden hair the same shade as their mother's. Although his pretty boy features were very much those of his father, Richard Sinclair, Alan's hazel eyes were identical to their mother's and contained a sharp, wary expression. He held a hardback book open in his hands and bent a corner to mark his place before closing it.

"Jack, this is a surprise." Alan's gaze switched to Nikki and he offered a congenial smile. "And Nikki. How lovely to see you again, if a trifle unexpected. You should have called to let me know you planned to visit, Jack."

"Should have. Didn't." He gestured toward the living room. "Let's talk."

"Would you care to join me for a drink?" Alan asked, starting toward the liquor cart.

"No, thanks. Have a quick question for you."

"And what would that be?"

"You stopped by Carolina Shipping around four the day Reginald was murdered. Mind telling me why?"

Alan gave a short laugh of disbelief. "You drove

all the way out here to ask me that? You should have phoned, Jack. It would have saved you a wasted trip."

But then he wouldn't have been able to see Alan's expression when they spoke. "You haven't answered my question."

"It's been so long, I'm not sure I even remember that day." Alan crossed to the couch and took a seat, placing one leg over the other in studied nonchalance. "Oh, of course. I recall now. I stopped by at some point that afternoon to invite you to dinner. But you were caught up in some big project and I didn't want to interrupt you."

"Dinner, Alan? That's a first. I don't remember you ever inviting me out before."

His brother picked up his glass and smiled over the rim, a hint of maliciousness peeking through. "If it helps reconcile you to the idea, I was going to make you pay."

"I don't doubt it." Jack continued to watch him, not disappointed to see his brother stir with the first signs of discomfort, nervously smoothing a wrinkle from the razor-sharp pleat of his trousers. "And while you were inviting me to dinner you just, what? Decided to call Dad from my building? Seems odd you didn't use your cell phone."

"I couldn't use my cell. The battery died."

"Why did you call Dad?"

Alan reached for his cigar, tapped away an expanse of ash and took a slow puff. "Since you weren't available for dinner I thought Reginald might join me. But as it turns out, he wasn't available." He shrugged. "I guess he had an appointment with a murderer."

Jack saw red. No doubt that was the intent. Swearing, he reached down, wrapped his fist in his brother's collar and jerked him to his feet. The cut glass tum-

bler crashed to the floor, along with the cigar, fling-
ing ice chips, bourbon and a flurry of sparks in a wide
semicircle.

Nikki returned the cigar to the ashtray then joined
Jack, sliding her hand across his bicep in a soothing
motion. "Let him go," she said quietly. "Hitting him
isn't going to solve anything."

"It might not solve anything, but it sure as hell will
make me feel better."

"All that will do is prove to Nikki what sort of man
you are," Alan asserted. "How you loved lording it over
me when Reginald forced his way back into Mother's
life. Until then you were nothing more than an un-
wanted bastard. My father despised you. Mother told
me so. Despised having you use the Sinclair name and
being forced to claim you for his own. Despised having
his legitimate son raised in association with filth. We
were happy, the three of us. The perfect family, except
for you trying to horn your way in. If Daddy hadn't
died, none of this would have happened."

It revolted Jack to hear the full extent of the poison
festering inside his brother, to have never suspected
the scope and depth of his hatred. "You're right, Alan.
Considering Richard was a man of modest means, you
wouldn't have all this." He swept his hand in a wide
arc to indicate their luxurious surroundings. "My father's money wouldn't have paid for that bourbon you
guzzle, or that Cuban cigar you're puffing on. Or en-
abled you to spend nearly thirty years freeloading off
his money. What happened, Alan? Did Dad threaten to
cut you off? Did he insist you get a job? Demand you
find your own place?"

"No! He loved me. Adored me." Alan's furious gaze

switched to Nikki. "You need to get away from him as soon as possible. He's not a safe man to be around."

"I know exactly what sort of man Jack is." Nikki tilted her head to one side. "What sort of man are you, Alan? Or maybe you've already answered that question."

He drew back a pace, surprised by her unexpected attack. "What the hell do you mean?"

"I mean… Where were you the night Reginald was murdered."

Alan's mouth dropped open. "I *beg* your pardon!"

"I'm just curious. You were in Charleston that night—"

"I most certainly was not," he denied indignantly. "I was right here. I left the city when it became clear Jack wasn't available for dinner."

"Or Reginald."

His mouth tightened. "Or Reginald. I decided to return home. When Reginald Kincaid met his unfortunate demise, I was right here with Mother. She held dinner for me. We watched TV for a time and then went to bed shortly before midnight. Not that I owe either of you any sort of explanation."

In the distance a key rattled in the lock and a moment later the door opened. "Alan?" Angela's voice came from the direction of the foyer. "I'm home."

"Your timing couldn't be better," Alan announced, glaring at Jack and Nikki. "Now you'll see how ridiculous your suspicions are."

Angela appeared in the doorway. Her surprised gaze landed on her two sons and then Nikki. She wore a set of light green surgical nursing scrubs, her hair twisted into a classic knot at her nape. She was a lovely woman with a figure more matronly than Elizabeth's, though it didn't detract from her overall classical beauty. She reminded Nikki a bit of Grace Kelly in her later years.

"Jack?" she asked uncertainly, stepping into the room. "What's going on?"

"Just having a discussion with my brother."

Angela released a tired sigh that crept into her eyes and dragged at her posture. "I wish you two would learn to get along."

"He thinks I killed Reginald," Alan claimed. He crossed the room to stand at his mother's side and wrapped an arm around her so they presented a unified wall. "Tell them what you told the police. That I was here with you at the time Reginald died."

Angela stiffened, her shocked gaze flashing to Jack. "You can't be serious. You can't honestly suspect—"

Jack stared at his mother, willing her to tell him the truth. "Was he here, Mom?"

She hesitated then shifted her footing, no doubt thrown off balance by Alan's overly possessive hold. She steadied herself with a hand to his chest. "Of course he was here. I told the police that, didn't I?"

"Actually, I didn't realize you had," Jack said quietly. "You never mentioned anything about it."

"Why would you think Alan might have killed Reginald?" Her eyes seemed to plead with him. "What in the world would make you think such a horrible thing?"

"He was in Charleston that afternoon."

"And?"

"And he called Dad on the phone from my office a couple of hours before the murder."

"As I said," Alan interrupted. "To invite him to dinner when you weren't available."

"That's it?" she asked, tears of relief welling into her

eyes. "You…you'd accuse your own brother of murder based on such flimsy evidence?"

Jack debated asking about the Indiana Jones style hat, but decided against it. There was no proof his brother owned one. And there was no point in tipping too much of his hand. In fact, he regretted coming here at all, for alerting Alan to his suspicions. But at the time Jack had made the decision, rational thought hadn't factored very strongly into the equation. Besides, he knew damn well what Alan would do if confronted by the police. He'd shift the blame.

Considering he'd gone out of his way to do precisely that by somehow stealing the Aston Martin and setting the scene to point in Jack's direction, more was needed than a nonexistent hat before going to the police. The phone call made from Carolina Shipping simply wasn't enough evidence, especially if Alan had their mother for an alibi. Time to stage a graceful retreat.

"I'm sorry, Mom. I didn't realize he was with you." He forced every ounce of sincerity he could muster into his voice. "I apologize, Alan. Seriously."

"And well you should," Alan said. Relief vied with righteous indignation.

"I guess I'm still more upset than I realized over Dad's death and it's making me a little crazy." Jack returned his glass to the liquor cart and glanced at Nikki. "We need to leave now."

She simply nodded.

He approached his mother and eased her from Alan's hold, kissing her cheek. "I'll call you in a few days."

"Yes. Yes, that would be fine."

He offered his brother an apologetic look. "Alan."

Alan smiled in triumph. "Jack."

Jack didn't speak again until they were in the car

and pulling out of the driveway. "It's not my imagination, is it? He killed Dad."

"Yes, Jack. He killed your father." Nikki stared out the front windshield, her mouth set in a grim line. "Now we just have to find a way to prove it."

"Here's a thought…"

Nikki rolled over in bed and rested her head on Jack's chest. When they'd first turned in, darkness held the room in a firm grip, but over the past hour, the moon peeked coyly above the horizon and cast its soft glow into the room, its silvery touch adding a brilliance to certain sections of the room while leaving the rest in mysterious shadow.

Five full days had gone by during which they'd endlessly examined various possibilities to explain Alan's alibi, as well as how he'd gotten his hands on Jack's car. They'd reluctantly concluded that Angela had lied to protect Alan. But they still couldn't figure out how to explain his use of Jack's car.

He ran a hand down Nikki's back in an absentminded caress. Unfortunately, there was nothing absentminded about her reaction to the stroking touch. "My main concern is that since Alan's my brother, it'll strengthen your detective buddy's suspicion that we're in on the murder together."

"But it would be downright stupid for you to give Alan your car while he's off committing a murder. Not when he could have rented something nondescript that the police couldn't connect to either of you. They might never have put his presence on that video together with the murder if Brooke hadn't remembered his overall appearance so clearly. He couldn't have anticipated that happening."

"Wait. Rewind."

"Where? What?"

"Alan could have rented something nondescript," Jack repeated slowly.

Nikki nodded. "Exactly. The only reason he didn't was in order to implicate you."

"Right, right. But… What if he didn't rent something nondescript? What if he rented a car identical to mine? What if he never took my car that night, just grabbed the license plates when he came to the office and stuck them on another car? What if it wasn't my car in that video, but a rental with my tags?"

"Oh, Jack. Is that possible?" She thought about it, the idea so out of left field it took her a minute to construct a reasonable counterargument. "That's a pretty distinctive car," she said slowly. "Not to mention pricey. What do those things run, anyway?"

"A couple hundred and up."

She stared, openmouthed. "Jack, that's obscene."

"Yes," he said with ripe male satisfaction.

"Would a rental company even carry that particular model and color? I'm not sure I'd want to let one of those off the lot."

He shrugged. "Shouldn't be too difficult to find out. There are companies who rent exotic cars. I'm not sure how many, though, or whether this particular make and model would be one of—" He broke off and shot up in bed. "Son of a bitch. Why didn't I think of this before?"

"What?" She sat up in alarm. "Think of what? What's wrong?"

"My car. Some idiot backed into the rear driver door two days before Dad's death. I forgot all about it."

"No doubt because you had a few other matters on your mind," she suggested gently.

He grimaced. "That's entirely possible. Still… I had the car repaired the next week. But, if we're lucky—and I mean very lucky—maybe that video will help prove that Aston Martin at the parking lot the night Dad was murdered isn't my car. I guess it didn't occur to me to ask Charles McDonough if the video showed the dent because I assumed it was my car." He turned to her, urgency sweeping through him. "We need to call him first thing tomorrow."

She shook her head. "Not tomorrow." At his blank look, she released her breath in exasperation. "It's your brother's wedding, remember?"

"Matt's not my brother," he instantly replied. But she couldn't help noticing it contained far less heat and conviction than in the past. His expression turned brooding and he settled back against the pillows. "Do you wake up Charles or should I?"

"I'll do it."

Nikki sat up and turned on the bedside lamp. A soft glow encompassed them, a circle of light holding the dense shadows at bay. She punched in the number, waiting for Charles McDonough's gravely bark at being awakened so late. Instead, the call went to voice mail. She gave a swift sketch of their theory and asked that he call at his earliest convenience.

"He's out of town until tomorrow afternoon," she informed Jack.

Jack frowned. "I guess a short delay won't hurt anything. I guarantee, Alan's not going anywhere, not when he can live in the lap of luxury at Mom's. Or rather, freeload in the lap of luxury. We'll go see Charles immediately after the wedding. With luck, he'll tie up his murder investigation before the annual shareholders' meeting."

Nikki froze. Praying Jack didn't pick up on her tension, she said, "That's the end of next week, isn't it?"

"Yes." He glanced at her, his blue eyes narrowing. "Have you tracked down our secretive stock owner, yet?"

She so did not want to take their conversation in this new direction. "I'll have the information before the meeting," she promised evasively.

"There aren't many days left. Just another week. And I'll need to have enough time to get them on my side." He sat up, frustration carved into his expression. "Unfortunately, I'm not certain whether I can pull that off. I mean, how am I supposed to convince someone that I'm the best choice to lead TKG when I'm under suspicion for murder? When my own brother is most likely responsible?"

"The Kincaids aren't going to blame you for Alan's actions. I'm sure this stockholder won't, either."

"No?" Jack ripped aside the bedcovers and paced across the room. Moonlight played over his magnificent physique, giving delicious definition to the endless ripple of muscles, painting them in streaks of silver and shadow. No question about it. Nudity became him. "I'm not so sure I'd be as accepting of the Kincaids' role in Dad's death if our situation were reversed."

"But none of you are to blame. There's no reason you can't reconcile with—"

"Don't."

That single word, spoken with such acute pain and explicitness, caused her to fall silent. Without a word, she left the bed and approached. "I'm just trying to help."

"We've already settled this issue, Nikki. Don't help

me. Not with the Kincaids. I don't want you interfering."

His words cut sharp and deep. In desperate need of fresh air, she opened the doors leading onto the deck and stepped outside, not caring that she didn't have a stitch on. She crossed to the railing and rested her hands on it, staring out at the ocean. The moon had escaped its watery bed, radiant in its fullness and shedding its light across the untamed landscape. Marsh grasses tilted beneath a gentle breeze, while wild sea oats stood sentry duty along the dunes, intent on their job of stabilizing the sand against the capricious winds that so often battered the coastline. Their laden heads bobbed against each other and she could just make out their dry, raspy whispers.

The landscape at night appeared so different from during the daytime, the sweet radiance of silver light softening sand, dunes and ocean. Nikki wanted to absorb the beauty before her, tuck it away somewhere safe to be taken out when her time with Jack was over. Tears pricked her eyes. They were down to mere days now. Seven. Seven days before she'd be forced to confess her role in The Kincaid Group's future. Seven days before he turned from her. Despised her. Cut himself off from her. She didn't know how she'd handle that moment when it came.

She sensed his presence a second before his hand cupped her shoulder. "You were made for moonlight," he told her, unwittingly echoing her earlier thoughts about him. "Almost as much as you were made for nudity. Every time I see you like this I think of the goddess Diana."

"The huntress. Goddess of the moon. Goddess of

childbirth." Nikki released a heartbreaking laugh. "She was committed to remaining a maiden, unlike me."

Jack's soft laugh rumbled against her back. "Thank God you weren't."

Her mouth twitched and she leaned against him. "She must not have met anyone like you or she wouldn't have remained a maiden for long."

Gently, inexorably, he turned her to face him. "Nikki, I know you want me to form a close relationship with my Kincaid relatives. But you need to know that's not going to happen. Ever."

"I do know."

He shook his head. "But you keep hoping."

She turned her back to the ocean and searched his face, his expression fully exposed by the moonlight, while hers remained in shadow. "Is that so wrong?"

"Not wrong. Pointless. Especially if—when—our relationship changes."

She froze, the breath stuttering in her lungs. Did he know? Had he guessed? "Changes?"

He must have caught some hint of her agitation because he smiled. Taking her left hand in his, he slipped a ring on her finger. Endless seconds ticked by before her brain absorbed what he'd done. He tilted her hand so it caught the moonlight, reflecting off a circle of glittering diamonds that surrounded a huge sapphire.

"Marry me, Nikki."

Her brain closed down. So did her capacity for speech. He must have taken her muteness for consent because he pulled her into his arms and covered her mouth with his. There beneath a benevolent moon, he kissed her with a passion that didn't allow room for thought. Unable to resist, she encircled his neck with her arms and gave herself up to rapture.

She barely felt her feet leave the deck, barely registered their transition from outdoors to in. Even when the softness of his mattress rose up to support her, she could only sigh against his mouth, opening to him more completely than she ever had before. How long had she loved him? How long had she hoped that a miracle would happen and he would fall in love with her, too? For reasons she couldn't quite summon to mind, the possibility of an engagement, of marriage, of creating a home with Jack and bearing his children had seemed an impossible dream. But in this moment out of time, she allowed herself to dream, to be swept off to a place where fantasies became reality. In the far distance darkness stole across the glorious horizon, a darkness she turned from.

Later. Later she'd deal with the darkness. But for now, she'd step into the light and grab hold of the gift that had fallen so delightfully and unexpectedly into her hands.

Threading her fingers through Jack's hair, Nikki pulled him downward so he fell into her mouth and onto her body. Oh, God, could anything be more delicious than that delectable joining of lips, of the abrasive, unmistakably male hardness moving against her softer, more giving curves? She opened to him, his tongue tangling with hers while his hands shaped her breasts and teased her nipples with quick, urgent little tugs.

He eased back from the kiss, drifted downward to replace his hands with his mouth. "You have the most beautiful breasts I've ever seen."

A strangled laugh escaped her. "I never know how to respond when you say something like that. Am I supposed to thank you? Say nothing? Deny it?"

"You can't deny the truth." He shifted lower, nipping at the flat planes of her belly. "And then there's your skin. Like cream. Not quite white, not tanned or leathery like some women who spend too much time in the sun."

She choked on a another laugh. "Heaven forbid."

"But a lovely, rich cream. And tasty." He inched lower. "I want another taste."

He slid his hands beneath her thighs and parted her. Then he did just as he'd promised and tasted. "Jack!" His name escaped in a breathless shriek.

She wanted to tell him to stop, that it was too intimate. But the gentle, insistent probing of his tongue and mouth drove every thought from her head and she could only feel. Feel that delicious roughness of whiskers and tongue, feel the hot tension build, feel the heat and desperate need pooling between her thighs. And then he found the small bud that was the source of all that need and tension. Found it. Caught it between his teeth. And tugged.

Nikki instantly splintered, coming apart in his hands. She arched upward, her fingers fisting in the sheets while her muscles drew bowstring taut. Air squeezed from her lungs and she shuddered as her climax slammed through her. It held her in its grip, refusing to let go, pulsating through her in an endless wave. Her nerve endings jittered to a dance unlike anything she'd ever experienced before and she felt like a swimmer who'd gone under for the count, her vision darkening while she struggled to breathe where no air existed.

She managed one long inhalation before Jack levered upward and in one swift thrust mated their bodies. Her body instantly tightened, started the swift build all over again. She wrapped him up in arms and legs and clung with all her might. She picked up the rhythm he set, meeting him thrust for thrust, desperately reaching for that pinnacle once again.

Jack's breathing deepened, quickened. So did their movements. Perspiration turned their bodies slick with need and heat, intensifying the abrasive slide of skin against skin. She heard him chanting "moremoremoremore" and found herself giving him more, as much as she had to give. She'd never been so open, so free, so desperate to meet demand with demand. And still they climbed and still the desire built until there was no place else for it to go. He surged inward a final time at the same moment she rose to meet him. They froze, held there like a pair of living statues captured at the perfect moment of climax, teetering on the brink of release. And then the tidal wave struck, washing over and through them, tumbling them onto the bed in a confusing heap of tangled limbs and pounding hearts and breath exploding in helpless gasps.

Jack groaned against her ear, the unexpected blast of heat causing her to shudder. She'd never been so hypersensitive before, not to the extent that even something as simple as his breath against her skin felt like the most delicious form of torture.

"What the hell happened?" he demanded. "I've never…"

"Never?"

"Not ever. You?"

"Not even close. Not within a million miles of what just happened."

He flopped onto his back. "I should have proposed sooner."

His words caused her to stiffen. All of a sudden the darkness invading her fantasy world crept closer. Much, much closer. "Jack…"

"Right here." The words were slurred and he rolled toward her and dropped a possessive arm across her waist. "I think you killed me."

"Jack, we need to talk."

In response he gave a soft snore. One glance warned he'd gone out like a light. The blanket of sleep must have been as king-size as the bed because she could feel it settling around her, too. She lifted her hand to look at the engagement ring. Over the past hour it had gained substantial weight since for some reason she could barely lift her arm. She stared at it, the promise it stood for mocking her with its brilliant flashes of diamond, silver and sapphire-blue.

She had no right to this ring. No right to wear it when she knew their marriage would never take place. Tears filled her eyes. She should have told him. She should have told him from the start that she owned those shares. And when he asked her to throw her shares in with his? Their affair would have ended because she'd have told him she couldn't. Wouldn't.

Her hand dropped to her side and her eyes fluttered closed. At least she had the past three months, something she wouldn't have experienced if she'd told him. And she had the rest of the night before she'd be forced to return the ring. The rest of the night to dwell within her fantasy world where Jack loved her and they were engaged. Where marriage hovered on the horizon instead of dark threat. Where the soft shades of their future children gamboled across the sweep of grass that surrounded his Greenville plantation. Where happiness dwelled, the only place it could dwell since it wouldn't survive outside of her fantasy.

Sleep claimed her. But just beforehand came the unsettling realization that not once in all the time she'd known Jack had he ever said he loved her. Thought almost woke her. The tear that escaped almost had her resurfacing.

Instead, she retreated into fantasy.

Eight

Something was wrong.

Jack couldn't quite put his finger on it, but at some point between the amazing passion they'd shared and the strident glare of morning light, Nikki had changed. She sat beside him, staring out of the front windshield of his Aston Martin, her hands wrapped tightly around a metallic sequined clutch, which hid her engagement ring from view. The electric-blue sequins matched those on her dress, a light smattering that started at her hip and dusted her silk dress like brilliant stars against a pale blue sky.

"What's wrong?" he asked quietly.

"What?" Startled from her reverie, she forced out a smile that didn't quite reach her eyes. "Oh, nothing. I guess I'm still half asleep."

He considered letting it go at that, then decided to press a little harder. "Seriously. What's wrong?"

The silence stretched for endless minutes. "This isn't a good time, Jack," she finally said in a low voice. "We're on our way to Matt's wedding. Why don't we talk afterward?"

"Talk. That means there is something wrong."

She released her breath in a long sigh. "Will Alan be at the wedding?"

More than anything he wanted to pull the car over and demand she tell him what the bloody hell was going on. He stewed for a full mile. "Yes, I'm sure Alan will be here, if only to reassure himself that we no longer suspect him. Considering your current attitude, we have every chance of success since he'll assume you've begun to suspect me of my father's death, instead of him." He paused. "Have you?"

"Don't be ridiculous." She spoke with such vehemence he had no choice but to believe her. "You could no more kill Reginald than I could."

"Okay. Good. Fine."

"What about Angela? Will she attend?"

It was a deliberate change of subject and Jack reluctantly went along with it. "Yes, just like she attended Kara and Eli's wedding, though I suspect it's the last place she wanted to be. It's not easy playing the 'other woman.'"

"No, I'm sure it isn't. It takes a lot of grit—a characteristic she passed onto her eldest son, if not her youngest."

Jack wanted to turn the conversation back to whatever had upset Nikki, but they'd arrived at the Colonel Samuel Beauchamp House, the use of Lily's home her gift to the bridal couple. The irony of the venue didn't escape him any more than it did Nikki. They'd met here. He'd stood on the balcony off the master bedroom salon when she'd entered the garden that night and bid a cool thousand for the pleasure of a dinner date with him... and the added bonus of a single wish. Then she'd disappeared into the darkness with him in pursuit. He'd caught up with her near the carriage house not far from where today's nuptials would take place. The instant they'd touched, they'd fallen headlong into passion. And when they'd exchanged their first kiss, there within the intimate embrace of a dark winter night, that passion had exploded out of control.

Nothing had changed since then. If anything, it had grown more intense, built to a level Jack knew he'd never share with another woman...had no interest in sharing with another woman.

"You never made your wish," he mentioned.

Nikki spared him a short, bleak look. "I'm saving it. I have a feeling I'm going to need it before much longer."

Seriously. What the *hell* was going on? He fought back a surge of impatience, battling against instincts that demanded he force the issue, regardless of time or place. He clung to his few remaining scraps of patience. "That sounds ominous," he limited himself to saying, downright impressed with his calm, easygoing tone.

"Not ominous, just true."

They exited the car and Jack reached for Nikki's hand. That's when he saw it—or rather, didn't see it. The ring finger of her left hand was bare. He froze and every last ounce of patience vanished in a surge of raw fury. Calm evaporated. As for easygoing... Screw easygoing. He'd never been easygoing in his life. Why start now?

"Where is it?" The words escaped low and harsh, far harsher than he'd intended.

She flinched. "I didn't think it wise to wear it today."

There was only one explanation for her newfound wisdom. She came from Charleston elite. He was a bastard, not to mention a murder suspect. "You're ashamed of our engagement." He threw the statement at her like a gauntlet.

"No! I...I'm just not sure there's going to be an engagement. At least, not yet. Not until we have a serious talk." She faced him, her eyes dark and shadowed with pain. "Jack, all this has caught me by surprise."

He held up her bare hand. "Yeah, all this has caught me by surprise, too." No matter what she claimed, she wouldn't be hedging over their engagement unless she distrusted him on some level. Was it the murder... or merely who and what he was? "What's going on, Nikki?"

She tugged free of his grasp. "Please not here. Not now."

He planted his size fourteens in the sweeping driveway and refused to budge. "Oh, hell, yes, sweetheart. Right here. Right now."

Her mouth set in a stubborn line. "Do you realize in the four months I've known you that you've never once said you love me?"

"Let me count the number of times you've said those words." He held up his hands as though to count. "Huh. Unless my addition's off, it's the same number of times I've told you."

She spared a swift look toward the house, taking in the stream of guests, some of whom had paused to watch their argument. Her breath escaped in a painful sigh. "Jack, I've been in love with you almost from the moment we met," she confessed in a low voice.

"Then why have you never said so?"

"Probably for the same reason you haven't. We've both been hurt. I told you about Craig. About how he used me. It makes it very difficult for me to say the words. I can also understand, based on your parents' affair, that you might have a rather unfortunate view of love, as well."

"Unfortunate view. An interesting way of putting it."

"But when you proposed… Why didn't you tell me you loved me then?"

"We got a little distracted."

A brief, reminiscent smile came and went. "That's true."

Jack dropped his hands to Nikki's shoulders. "Sweetheart, I love you. I wouldn't ask you to marry me if I didn't." His declaration provoked tears. He gently thumbed the moisture from her cheeks. "Don't. Not when I just told you I love you."

"I have a confession to make," she said in a low voice. "And when I make it you won't love me anymore."

He stiffened, uncertain how to respond to that. He'd been aware, ever since Charles McDonough came to his beach house, that she was keeping something from him. Now he'd find out what. "Nikki," he began in concern.

"Trouble in paradise?" Alan's question came as an unwelcome interruption. He approached, his expression settling into lines of deep concern. "I did warn you about my brother, Nikki." He managed to hit the perfect blend of sorrow and indignation. "Jack's not a safe man to be around. I can escort you out of here, if you'd like. He won't stop us with everyone watching."

"Not now, Alan," Jack bit out.

His brother ignored him and held out his hand to Nikki. "I'm here for you, my dear."

She took a swift, instinctive step backward. "Not a chance in hell," she told him.

Alan's hand dropped stiffly to his side and embarrassment reddened his cheeks at the slight. He glanced around, fury replacing his embarrassment when he realized how much attention they'd attracted. Without a word, he spun on his heel and walked away.

"Oh, God, I shouldn't have done that," she whispered. "We were trying to allay his suspicions and all I've done is make them worse. I just couldn't help it. When he reached for me all I could see was the hand of a murderer."

Jack sighed. "Don't worry about it. You weren't going anywhere with him. I wouldn't have let you. So even if you hadn't rejected him, I would have reacted, and more forcefully than you. I also doubt that anything we could have said or done today would have eased his suspicions. It was ridiculous of me to think we could. Just as nothing I did during our childhood was sufficient to create a fraternal bond between us."

"Not even saving his life?"

"That only made it worse, especially when I didn't cooperate and die."

Nikki flinched. "Don't say that."

"You do realize that if I hadn't saved him that day, Reginald would still be alive."

She turned on him, hands planted on her hips, eyes flashing like the sapphire in the engagement ring she wasn't wearing. "Except that the guilt of standing by and doing nothing would have eaten you alive. You wouldn't be the man you are today if you'd allowed your brother to die. That's not who you are, Jack."

Did she have any idea how much her vehement defense meant to him? She couldn't possibly realize how those three simple sentences of support cut straight through to his marrow, gutting him. So few people in his life had shown such keen understanding of who he was at the very core. In part it was because he kept himself aloof from others, distancing his emotions and barricading all vulnerabilities from possible attack or harm.

He'd learned the importance of that at school, when he'd been subjected to various slights and slurs once his illegitimacy came to light—and Alan made certain it came to light on a regular basis. Girls had been warned away from him, as though he carried something they might catch. Boys sneered at his bastard status. Like tended to gravitate to like and there were damn few kids like him. Though the taint had followed him to college, the facts surrounding his birth weren't as relevant, anymore, until gradually it hadn't mattered at all. At least, it wasn't relevant to what he'd accomplished with his life. But those early years had left an indelible mark.

"Nikki…" He wanted to explain it to her, explain how those experiences made him sensitive to slights— such as her refusing to wear his engagement ring in front of Charleston's elite. But the faint strains of music issuing from the back of the mansion warned they were out of time. Regret swept through him and he forced himself to set it aside. He cupped her elbow, urging her toward the spacious patio and garden. "Come on. Let's do our duty and then get the hell out of here."

He paused to give his mother a kiss before taking a seat behind her and Alan, who sat at attention, refusing to look at them. Not that Jack objected. He'd had more than enough of his brother for one day.

The ceremony was lovely, or so everyone claimed. Since he was no expert, he wasn't in a position to debate the issue. In his opinion his three Kincaid sisters, who acted as Susannah's attendants, looked beautiful in their halter top dresses. The bride was downright stunning, her slender figure showcased in a strapless gown. It molded to her hips before flowing outward in a long, sweeping train. Matt appeared poleaxed by her, a suitable expression for a man about to be married.

The opening chords of the processional drifted across the gathering and three-year-old Flynn walked his mother up the aisle. Someone had slicked his dark hair down but hadn't quite managed to keep the bow tie of his little tux from being knocked askew. But most moving of all was seeing him beam from ear to ear, his adoring gaze shifting from his father to his mother. And when the couple eventually exchanged their vows— ones they'd written themselves—the emotional words stirred tears in a good portion of those assembled.

The ceremony didn't take long, fortunate since the cooling breeze flagged just enough for a subtle wave of humidity to seep through. "I assume we have to stick around for a while?" Jack asked in an undertone, hoping against hope that Nikki would insist they leave right away.

She instantly dashed those hopes. "For at least an hour."

"Hell."

His mother joined them. Behind her, Jack caught a glimpse of Alan's retreating back. "Would you mind if I stay at the beach house tonight?" she asked, her face pale and drawn.

"Problem?"

She shrugged. "Alan's in one of his moods. We could probably both use a break from each other's company. I'm not due back to work until Monday, so I thought we could spend a little time together." She offered Nikki a smile, a genuine one, Jack was relieved to note. "The three of us, of course."

"I'd enjoy that," Nikki replied with an equally genuine smile.

"You're welcome to stay as long as you want, Mom," he assured her. "We're going to cut out in about an hour. I'll track you down when it's time."

"Thanks. I guess I better go be sociable." She spared a glance toward the cluster of Kincaids and sighed. "Even if it kills me."

Over the next hour, Jack kept a discreet eye on his watch, counting down the minutes until they could leave. He popped a small round puffball of some sort in his mouth before glancing at his watch yet again. Ten more minutes. Ten more minutes and they'd be out of here. He could handle another ten.

Maybe.

He also kept an eye on Alan, who'd shed his affable facade and revealed a hint of a more familiar petulance. It didn't bode well for the future since that petulance often led to his lashing out, without considering the consequences. Jack debated whether or not to talk to him in an attempt to smooth over troubled waters before they grew any more turbulent. Before he could, Nikki touched his arm.

"Jack, look."

She drew his attention to Elizabeth who sat at a table with Cutter, the two chatting with her three daughters. Harold Parsons, the family attorney, approached. He took his time greeting each in turn, no doubt showing the kindness and courtly charm he reserved for the Kincaids, versus the more irascible attitude Jack had experienced. After a few minutes of chitchat, he held out a familiar looking envelope, The Kincaid Group's distinctive logo decorating one corner. It was identical to the letter Jack had received at the reading of the will—the one his father had left to him and which he had yet to open. While Jack's sealed letter was heavily creased and careworn from frequent handling, a coffee ring stain marring its surface, Elizabeth's appeared pristine.

"He's apologizing," Nikki murmured.

"Son of a bitch, he had it all along."

Elizabeth said something that appeared to be a question, her head tilting to one side. In response, Harold gestured in Jack's direction. Almost as one, the four women swiveled to look at him, open shock on the faces of his three sisters, an expression of intense gratitude on Elizabeth's. She excused herself and disappeared in the direction of the carriage house, no doubt to read her letter in private.

Jack frowned. "I wonder what it says? I hope it's something nice. If Dad was as cruel to her in the letter as he was the night he died—"

"Reginald wouldn't do that," Nikki insisted.

Elizabeth reappeared a few minutes later. The girls fluttered around her in a flurry of questions and concern. She spoke at some length before excusing herself and heading in their direction, her eyes fixed on Jack.

"Oh, man." He waited, grim-faced, prepared to take whatever Elizabeth planned to dish out.

To his shock, she dished out a tight hug and a lingering kiss on his cheek. "Thank you," she told him, her voice choked with tears.

Over her shoulder Jack caught a glimpse of Alan who stared at the embrace in stunned disbelief—disbelief that rapidly transitioned to outrage. He'd been so pleased by his own welcome into the Kincaid fold, quick to rub his open-ended Sunday dinner invitation in Jack's face. Alan had been even more pleased by the Kincaids open dislike of Jack and took every opportunity to mention it. No doubt this mending of the familial breech both shook and infuriated him.

Elizabeth started speaking and he transferred his attention to her, sliding the problem of his half brother to the back burner. "You have no idea how much this means to me. The fact that you're the one who insisted there had to be a letter…" She shook her head. "Oh, Jack. I was so certain Reginald had deliberately slighted me. Instead, he accepted full responsibility for his actions. He said just what you told me, that he'd been fortunate enough to love two women in his life and that he'd never meant to hurt me the way he had."

"I'm glad I could help." It was the only thing he could think to say. Apparently, it was the right thing.

She smiled. "You're very much like him, you know. Only you have a sense of integrity and honor that he sometimes lacked." She caught his hand in hers and gave it a tug. "Come over and join us. Get to know your sisters."

"They're not… I'd rather—" He shot Nikki a glance that clearly said "get me the hell out of this." Instead of getting him the hell out, she threw him to the wolf in sheep's clothing.

"Go on, Jack," Nikki encouraged. "It's long overdue."

"Yes, I insist." A thread of wolfish steel underscored Elizabeth's words.

Left without any other choice, he followed in her wake. He snagged Nikki's arm when she hung back.

"If I'm going down, you're going down with me," he informed her in a bitter undertone.

Laurel, Kara and Lily stood in a row, oldest to youngest, and looked like lovely flowers in their bridesmaid dresses. Though they'd all met before, Elizabeth introduced each in turn. Laurel was the image of her mother, with auburn hair and flashing green eyes, her coloring enhanced by her buttercup-yellow dress. Kara, the shortest of the three, wore an emerald-green that brought out a hint of bronze in her brown hair and blended nicely with her eyes. Someone had mentioned that she ran Prestige Events and had organized Matt and Susannah's wedding as her gift to them. Finally he turned his attention to Lily, a more vivacious version of her oldest sister with golden-red hair that curled down her back. She was clearly the outgoing one of the group as well as being in the final stages of pregnancy. A children's book illustrator, he vaguely recalled. Her dress matched her blue eyes and cascaded over her baby bulge.

"Thank you, thank you, thank you," she said, swooping over to give him a quick, energetic hug that pressed that huge, rather scary baby bump tight against him. "You have no idea how upset we've all been over Dad neglecting to write Mom a letter. I can't believe it didn't occur to any of us that it might simply have gone missing. And I can't tell you enough how much we appreciate the fact that it did occur to you."

Laurel, TKG's long-distance PR Director now that she'd married her husband, Rakin Abdellah, fixed Jack with a shrewd gaze. "Nikki was right all along. You're one of the good guys. You have no idea how relieved we all are to discover that."

"I'm not one of the good guys," he instantly denied.

He turned on Nikki. "You have to stop telling people I am. Why would you lie to people about that?"

While his Kincaid sisters laughed as though he'd said something funny, Nikki smiled. "Because you are a good guy."

Before he could prove otherwise, Lily chimed in. "We've been so worried about your intentions toward The Kincaid Group. Thank goodness we can put that concern to rest." Her hand rubbed distressing little circles across her distended belly, her wedding rings flashing in the sunlight. With luck her soothing touch would keep the kid right where it was until well after the reception. Jack opened his mouth to explain in no uncertain terms just how wrong she was when she added, "That sort of stress isn't good for the baby."

He clamped his back teeth together and altered course slightly. "There's still the outstanding ten percent," he warned. "Nothing's decided until we determine which way the final shareholder plans to vote."

Laurel offered a smile that appeared uncomfortably genuine. "True. Of course, if you throw your vote to RJ, those shares become moot."

Crap! Five sets of feminine eyes stared at him with various degrees of warmth, from Elizabeth's sweetness, to Laurel's friendliness, to Kara and Lily's delight, to Nikki's open relief. Her eyes filled with a distressing combination of love and tears while the mouth he couldn't seem to get enough of quivered into a hopeful grin.

How the hell did she do it? How the hell did she keep arranging events so he ended up on the receiving end of Kincaid gratitude? Well, it wouldn't last long. Not when they found out he had no intention of throwing his forty-five percent in RJ's corner. Then all those lovely smiles would fade and they'd rip him to shreds. At least then their relationship would return to normal.

"Time to go," he announced, slipping his hand under Nikki's elbow.

Before he could escape, the Kincaids descended once again, giving him an endless stream of farewell hugs and well wishes. He'd almost reached the breaking point when they finally let go. Without another word, he spun on his heel and moved at a rapid clip across the patio. Nikki had to practically run to keep up.

"Slow down, will you. And don't forget we need to collect your mother."

He turned on her. "No, I will not slow down, not until we're out of earshot of all those damn Kincaids." He continued moving until they rounded a corner and were clear of viewing and hearing range. "I warned you about interfering, Nikki. I told you I have no interest in establishing any sort of familial relationship with them. But did you listen? No."

She jerked her arm free of his hold. "Wait just one minute, bubba. That lovefest back there had nothing to do with me. You were the one who suspected Reginald left a letter for Elizabeth. You were the one who called Harold Parsons. And you were the one who didn't correct your sisters when they assumed you'd vote for RJ at the annual meeting."

"For the last time, they are *not* my sisters."

"You know something, Jack? I've had it with your denials. Whether you like it or not, they *are* your sisters. And the reason you didn't correct their assumption is because you didn't want to hurt them. Now quit dumping your B.S. on me and try smelling what you're so busy shoveling for a change. Until you do, I'm going home." She jabbed a finger to his chest to emphasize her final words. "Alone."

Spinning around, she struck off down the driveway toward the street. He stood there a minute, too stunned to move. What did she mean "try smelling what you're so busy shoveling"? He'd never been anything but completely up-front about his feelings toward his brothers and sisters—*not* his brothers and sisters. He lowered his head and swore beneath his breath. When had he started referring to them as brothers and sisters? Because somehow, at some point, that's precisely how he'd begun to feel about them.

Okay, maybe not RJ. But the others…

He knew how dangerous it was to open himself up like that. He was a bastard and nothing would ever change that. If they considered him kin, it was on those terms and those terms alone. It wasn't because they liked or respected him. They were simply stuck with him.

And yet… He couldn't help but recall Matt's friendly smile, and the way he'd greeted Jack today with a slap on the back and a one-armed hug. Of course, his brandnew marriage made him so euphoric he'd probably have done the same to a pink-haired baboon with bad breath and a coat full of fleas. And then there had been Elizabeth's effusive greeting. Also understandable considering her emotional state after reading the letter his father had left for her. Same with his sisters. They were so excited about the letter he'd been briefly swept into their circle of love.

Still…it felt good. Too good.

Jack shot his hands through his hair and groaned. How had it happened? When? Somehow a door opened and he didn't have a clue how to slam it shut again. Of course, it would slam shut at the annual board meeting. Then he'd see how chummy his "family" remained. Which brought him to his next problem.

He stared in the direction Nikki had taken. He refused to let her leave. Not until they straightened out a few vital details, such as why she refused to wear his ring. He'd also demand she tell him what secret she continued to keep from him. Not to mention forcing her to explain once and for all why she was so determined to reconcile him with the Kincaids. Granted, he'd also apologize for acting like a prize jerk. But something was going on here and he wanted to know what.

He reached the street and didn't see her. But if she was busy walking off her mad, he could make an educated guess which way she'd gone in order to return to her Rainbow Row home. He set off in that direction, moving at a ground-eating pace. Rounding the next corner, he saw her a couple of dozen feet ahead of him. She approached an alley running along the back of the homes occupying that block—including the Colonel Samuel Beauchamp House. The narrow access road connected to the main boulevard and she spared a quick glance toward the alley before starting across.

Jack heard the screech of tires the exact second Nikki did, her head jerking toward the alley. He couldn't say what warned him of her imminent danger. He simply knew that—like with Alan all those years ago—she was about to be hit by a speeding car. He didn't think. He broke into a flat-out run. A few paces ahead of him, Nikki froze, everything about her communicating intense alarm. He reached her a split second before the car and snatched her backward with such force they both hit the pavement, and hit hard.

They rolled toward the street and dropped into the

gutter. He tried to cushion the impact, but had a feeling she'd collected more than her share of scrapes and bruises. The car skidded around the corner onto the main street, so close he could feel the heat from the exhaust and the stinging kick of dirt and gravel. The engine gunned and it took off without stopping.

"Nikki!" His hands swept over her. "Sweetheart, how bad are you hurt?"

She trembled against him. "I'm…I'm okay. I think." She struggled to stand. If they'd been anywhere else other than in a filthy street, he'd have made her lie still while he examined her for injuries.

"No, not yet," he insisted. "Don't get up until I check you out."

Gently, he eased her to a sitting position on the edge of the curb and ran through a curtailed version of the basic A through E primary examination his mother had taught him. Nothing broken. No indication of a head injury. Just some general scrapes and bruises.

"Okay, you pass," he said in relief.

"Oh, Jack!" She threw her arms around his neck and clung.

"Easy. Easy, honey." He could feel the dampness of tears against his dress shirt. "What happened, do you know?"

"He came at me. He almost hit me. If you hadn't gotten there in time…" She began to cry in earnest.

"Who, Nikki? Did you see the driver?"

She pulled back a couple inches. A painful scrape rode her cheekbone and along her chin where the metallic sequins from her purse had connected with her face. "Oh, Jack. It was Alan. Alan tried to kill me."

Nine

By the time Nikki and Jack returned from the police station, she barely had enough energy to pull herself from the car.

Between her various aches and pains from her tumble to the street, and her mental and emotional exhaustion from the endless rounds of questions Charles McDonough had asked, all she wanted was to crawl into bed and pull the covers over her head. One look at Jack warned he felt the same way.

"Will your mother be okay?" she asked.

"Should be. McDonough said they wouldn't charge Mom for lying to cover for Alan, not if she testifies against him."

Deep lines of pain carved a pathway across his face. More than anything Nikki wished she could ease that pain, but there was nothing she could say or do that would change the reality that Jack's brother had killed his father. Worse, his mother had lied to protect the son she sincerely believed innocent.

In fact, it hadn't been until Charles had shown the video from the parking lot the night of the murder that the pieces fell into place. There was no dent on the Aston Martin that drove onto the lot, proving it couldn't have been Jack's car. Between the accident pictures he pulled off his cell phone, and the receipt for the repair provided after a single phone call to the mechanic, it became clear that the car in the video wasn't Jack's.

Even more damning was the hat and coat Alan wore that night. One look and Angela burst into tears. She'd bought Alan both items and finally confessed she had no idea what time Alan returned home that night since she'd fallen asleep on the couch while reading. When she awoke he'd been sitting in a nearby chair, also reading, and claimed he'd been there for hours. She had no reason to question his statement until recently.

By the time they left the station a warrant had been issued for Alan's arrest. Nikki suspected that once they checked his bank records and credit card statements, they'd find the necessary evidence proving he'd rented the same make and model car that Jack drove. Knowing Charles and his bulldog tendencies, it wouldn't take him long to build all the circumstantial evidence into a strong case against Alan.

"I just wish Mom could have come home with us," Jack said.

"Don't you think she'll be safer in protective custody until Alan's been apprehended? I hate the thought that he might go after her now."

"Mom's safety is one of the few points McDonough and I agree on, otherwise I'd have insisted they release her." He nudged Nikki toward the flight of stairs leading to the bedroom. "Come on. Maybe it won't seem so bad if we drag each other up."

Together they climbed, tugging off clothes as they went. By the time they hit the bedroom, they were both naked. Nikki beelined toward the bed, brought up short by the hard, powerful arm Jack wrapped around her middle. He swung her off her feet and headed for the bathroom.

"Shower first. I want to make sure all those abrasions get cleaned out again." Jack reached into the stall—a huge tiled expanse with multiple jets—and turned on the water. "Plus, it'll help take the edge off our poor aching muscles."

Hot, steamy water blasting out and Nikki stepped into the middle of the pulsating jets and groaned in sheer delight. "Oh, God, I just died and went to heaven."

"Brace yourself against the wall," he instructed. "I'll take care of the rest."

She followed his directions. She didn't think she could love him more, but the next few minutes proved her wrong. He carefully soaped every inch of her body, beyond gentle when he found and cleaned each scrape and abrasion. His hands kneaded the various bands of muscles from ankle to neck, his thumbs digging in and soothing tendons she didn't even realize had become knotted into throbbing tangles. And then he finished his self-appointed task by drawing her up for the sweetest of kisses, causing more knots to develop, but ones from a far different cause.

She wrapped her arms around him and lost herself in the steam from the shower and the more intense steam from his kiss. He fumbled behind her and the spray of water subsided. Somehow he found towels and wrapped them up in a delicious cocoon of damp bodies and soft cotton. She couldn't begin to imagine where he found the energy when she barely had enough to find the bed. He even managed to dry her with swift, brisk strokes that left her skin tingling, before applying the towel to himself. Together they fell into bed and into each other's arms.

"Will they find Alan?" she asked.

"Eventually." He tucked her against his side, a sweet alignment of curves and angles that fit together as they had from the start…with utter perfection. "I doubt Alan went home to Greenville, not once he calmed down and considered the ramifications of attempting to run you over. Since he missed, he had to suspect we'd go to the cops and report him. He also can't access much money from his bank account since it's the weekend. I guarantee Charles will have his funds frozen first thing Monday morning."

"It's not your fault, you know," she said gently.

Her comment caused lines to bracket Jack's mouth, grief settling into the deep grooves. She'd found the source of his pain and cut straight through to the heart of it. "I'm not sure the Kincaids will see it the same way."

"Reginald's murder was your brother's fault and no one else's. Not Angela's. Not Reginald's. And not yours. There's something wrong with Alan at the core." She rolled onto her hip and cupped Jack's face. Whiskers rasped against her palm in a tantalizing abrasion, while tension built along his jawline. "Reginald had six children and not one of them turned out like Alan. Every last one of you has made something of your life. Alan received the exact same benefits the rest of you did—more even than you were willing to accept. And he wasted the opportunity. He has the attitude that the world owes him a living instead of his owing the world for his existence and giving back in some productive way."

"Maybe if—"

Nikki shifted her hand so her fingertips covered his mouth. "Don't. All the 'what ifs' and 'maybes' in the world won't change anything and will only make it worse. We can't know what might have happened if we turned left instead of right. Gone backward instead of forward. Jumped instead of ducked. We can only deal with what is, not what might have been."

Jack's tension eased ever so slightly. "I would have stopped him if I'd known how sick he was."

"None of you realized the extent of it because he hid his true personality so well. Everyone thought Alan was charming. People liked him. I know I did, at least at first." She shrugged. "He has a talent for hiding the darkness inside."

Jack grimaced. "I knew it was there."

"Did you ever worry that he'd harm your mother or father?"

"No, of course—" His breath escaped in a long sigh and he pulled her close, simply holding her while he accepted the same truth his mother had. He hadn't wanted to believe Alan capable of such evil because he'd judged his brother by his own standards of decency and morality, standards Alan had rejected long ago. "No, of course not, or I'd never have left him alone in the house with my mother."

She hugged him tight. "And you would have warned your father."

Jack traced a finger along the curve of her cheek. "How do you do it?" he asked in a rough voice. "How do you manage to take something that's so dark and bleak and turn it around?"

She smiled. "I just show you the same problem from a slightly different angle. You do the rest."

"Like with my…my brothers and sisters?"

It was the first time she'd heard him use those terms of his own volition. She shut her eyes, tears pressing hard. She gave herself a few seconds to gather her control before replying. "That's right, Jack. I'd already met most of your family so I knew they were good people. It was only a matter of showing you that side of them."

"Well…most of them," he said with a sour edge. "The jury's still out on RJ."

Her laughter contained a hint of the tears she fought so hard to temper. Exhaustion. No doubt they came from exhaustion. "Then my job's almost done."

"It will be as soon as you uncover the missing shareholder."

She burrowed against him. She couldn't handle this. Not now. Not when she could barely keep her eyes open. A heavy bank of fatigue hit her with such force she couldn't even think straight. "Jack—"

Before she could say anything more, he kissed her, a kiss of passion tempered with tenderness. And though she shifted against him, eager for more, she could feel herself fading. The delicious taste of his kiss was the last thing she remembered before sleep claimed her, a lovely drifting into dreams where Jack held her safe and secure and all was well with their world.

She woke to another kiss, a kiss of tenderness edged with passion. Her instantaneous response hit before she fully surfaced, and she gave herself to Jack without hesitation. Her eyes flickered open at the same moment he mated their bodies and the air escaped her lungs in a soft gasp of delight. She couldn't imagine a better way to greet the morning and she moved with him, their rhythm one of sheer perfection.

Only a few more days. Just a handful. Just a handful left to change his mind about taking over The Kincaid Group. From taking revenge on brothers and sisters who'd never harmed him. How could she possibly get him to see this final problem from a different angle, to somehow turn it all around? Simple. She didn't. There wasn't an angle in the world that would convince him to hand the running of TKG over to RJ, any more than there was any possible angle which would make her ownership of those crucial TKG stock shares more palatable.

She pushed the worry aside and embraced the moment, her pain and fear lending a desperate urgency to her lovemaking. He must have picked up on it on some level because he caught fire, driving them higher, further, every stroke and caress burning with an incandescence they'd never experienced before. She literally felt as though he'd filled her with such brilliant passion she couldn't contain it all without bursting into flames. Recklessly, she threw herself into the fire and allowed it to consume her, all of her, building the pyre as high as it would go. And then she built it higher still.

It couldn't last. Together they hit the peak, teetered for the briefest of moments, before their climaxes ripped through them, a shattering so intense Nikki couldn't remember where she was or when…though the "who" in the equation remained crystal clear. Jack shuddered in her arms and collapsed on top of her.

"Fifty more years," he insisted.

She shook her head in confusion. "What?"

"I want fifty more years of that. Maybe sixty."

She laughed, even though her heart was breaking. "I'll see what I can do."

"Hot tub, shower or food? Since we have sixty more years, I can be generous and let you choose."

"Food. I'm starved. I can whip something together. Pancakes? Omelets? Grits?"

"Yes."

Nikki grinned. "Coming right up."

They ate out on the deck in their bathrobes, enjoying the warm breeze flowing off the ocean. She deliberately kept the conversation light and casual. They'd had so many dark issues to deal with the day before, she just wanted to kick back and relax. To pretend that their future held endless Sunday mornings like this one. Even as she wallowed in the pleasure of it she knew it wouldn't last.

And it didn't.

Jack took a long swallow of coffee, eyeing her through the steam rising from his drink. "Truth time, Nikki," he announced.

She paused with her cup halfway to her mouth. Carefully, she returned it to the saucer. Her heart rate kicked up. Did he know? Did he suspect? "What truth, Jack?"

"You didn't wear your engagement ring to Matt and Susannah's wedding yesterday. Why? Were you ashamed to admit to all your society friends that you'd agreed to marry me? Ashamed to admit it to the Kincaids?"

She immediately leaned forward and caught his hand in hers. "No!" she told him, filling that single word with absolute conviction. "That's not it at all. I've never cared about those things. It's not how I was raised."

"It would be understandable considering your mother's a Beaulyn," Jack suggested. "The crème de la crème of Charleston high society."

"Granted, my mother could have had her pick of any of the men within that sphere. But she loved my father—a cop—and that's who she married." More than anything Nikki wanted to reassure him on that point and a hint of urgency rippled through her response. "Do you really think she would have raised me to think any differently?"

"Then why didn't you wear my ring yesterday?"

She closed her eyes. The time had come. Selfishly, she thought she'd have a handful of days before admitting the truth. Now they slipped through her fingers like grains of windblown sand. Slowly, she released his hand. "Because I didn't want to agree to an engagement that's going to end almost as soon as it begins."

Jack shoved back his chair and stood, towering over her. "What the hell does that mean? What's going on, Nikki?"

She forced herself to give it to him straight. "I know who owns the final ten percent of TKG stock."

His eyes narrowed, anger flashing through the crystalline blue. "And you've already given the information to RJ?"

She shook her head. "He doesn't know."

That gave Jack pause. "Then why would you think I'd end our engagement over the missing shareholder, unless…" He stilled and she caught understanding dawning in his gaze. "Son of a bitch. It's you, isn't it?"

"Yes," she confessed. "I own the shares."

"All this time we've been involved—intimately involved—and you've kept this from me?"

She flinched at the outrage underscoring his question. "I think you can guess why."

"Oh, no guessing involved, sweetheart." Somehow he'd managed to turn the word "sweetheart" into a curse. "There can only be one reason. You don't trust me."

"It isn't a matter of trust," she instantly denied.

He cut her off with a sweep of his hand. "Bull! We met nearly five months ago. You had all the time in the world to tell me you were the shareholder in control of the final ten percent of TKG stock. I guarantee you would have been up-front about your ownership if you trusted me."

"It wasn't you I didn't trust, Jack." Time for utter honesty, no matter how miserable it made her. "It was what you would do with the information I couldn't trust."

He didn't pull his punches. "You mean what I might pressure you to do with those shares."

"Something like that," she admitted.

He paced to the railing, his long, impatient strides eating up the deck. "Let's start over." He turned and faced her. "How did you come into possession of the shares?"

"My grandfather, Todd Beaulyn, encouraged your father to expand into real estate. Reginald needed to borrow money in order to do so."

He thought it through. "I assume your grandfather provided the funds in exchange for ten percent stock in TKG?"

"Yes."

"And you then inherited the shares from Beaulyn, along with your Rainbow Row house?"

She nodded. "I was his only grandchild, and my mother wasn't interested in the house or the shares."

"That's quite an inheritance."

She kept her gaze steady on his. "It's also the other reason Reginald hired me when my career went south. Your father wanted me to understand the inner workings of TKG so I'd be able to make intelligent decisions about how to vote my shares when the time came. Of course, since he owned ninety percent to my ten percent, there wasn't much voting involved while he was alive."

"How is it possible that RJ doesn't know you own them?"

"Reginald didn't tell anyone he'd sold off a portion of the company in order to expand into the real estate market," she explained. "As part of the contract, my grandfather agreed to keep the sale confidential and buried ownership beneath several levels of holding companies. Granddad was a clever man. You'd have to know where to look to find it."

"No doubt Dad didn't want any flack from the family."

She shrugged. "Could be. When I inherited the shares, Reginald asked if I would also maintain the same confidentiality as my grandfather. I agreed."

"Of course, he had you over a barrel," Jack pointed out. "It's not like you would have refused considering he'd just saved your professional reputation by offering you a job."

"I would have remained silent, regardless," she insisted.

Jack leaned back against the railing and folded his arms across his chest, his eyes winter-cold. "Let's see if I have this straight. You worked for The Kincaid Group the entire time we've been together—without bothering to mention that fact to me. You've also owned the outstanding ten percent shares, also without bothering to mention it, and even knowing it was information I required in time for the board meeting. In other words, our entire relationship is founded on lies."

Exhaustion swept over her. "I didn't tell you about my connections to The Kincaid Group because I wanted to have a relationship with you. Once you found out the truth, our involvement would end. And you know why, Jack." Pain filled her at the undeniable fact that who she was would always come second to what she owned. That he would always want her more for those shares than for love. "The stock will always come between us because I hold the solution to your goal of destroying the Kincaids."

"If our relationship ends it's because you've kept secrets from a man you claim to love, not because of where you work or the stock you own."

Nikki shot to her feet. "I don't *claim* to love you. I do love you. What possible benefit is there for me in our relationship other than love? You made it clear from the start that you despised the Kincaids, that you intended to take them down and, no doubt, me with them. If I'd told you about the stock shares what would you have done?"

"Exactly what I intend to do now. Ask to buy your shares or have you give me your proxy, which is the same thing RJ will do."

"RJ wants them in order to preserve TKG. You want them so you can destroy the Kincaids," she shot back.

"I've already told you. I have no intention of destroying The Kincaid Group."

"Only the Kincaids."

She saw the split-second hesitation. The slightest crack in the fierce determination he'd shown up until now. She deliberately changed the subject in order to throw him off-kilter, hoping against hope she could get him to look at the situation from a fresh angle—one that might put an end to his ridiculous need for vengeance. "Why do you own this house, Jack? Why do you own the plantation in Greenville?"

He shook his head. "What the hell are you talking about?"

"How many bedrooms do you have, combined between the two places? A dozen? Two dozen? Three?"

"I never bothered to count."

"How many square feet?" She hammered him with the questions. "Ten thousand, twenty? More?"

Jack shot a hand through his hair, his irritation palpable. "What's your point, Nikki?"

"You bought homes, Jack. *Homes.*" She stressed the word, hoping against hope he'd pick up on the significance. "Homes which are meant for large families. And yet, there's just you. Well, and your mother and Alan," she felt obligated to add.

"They never lived with me."

She pounced on his statement. "Exactly. Your mother and Alan have—or rather, had—their own home. So, why didn't you buy some sort of ritzy two bedroom apartment overlooking the harbor? Why a home, Jack?"

"Stop using that word. They're not homes. They're houses. Investments."

She released her breath in a sigh. "I think some part of you knows differently. I think on an unconscious level you want to fill them with family, maybe because yours has always been so fractured. You could have that. You could have your family here."

"I don't want them."

"You're lying." She dared to step closer, urgency threading through her words and communicating itself in the tension of her body. "All these years you've believed you were on the outside, looking in. Instead, you've locked yourself away in homes crying out for a family and refused to open the door. Don't you get it, Jack? You're already inside. You just have to let others in here with you."

"Are you finished?" He'd closed down, ruthlessly cutting off access to any sort of emotional connection. "I'd like to settle our business issues."

"I'm not even close to finished. But since you want to discuss business, let's do that. Are you really going to take over the company your father spent all these years building, just so you can extract some sort of petty revenge by tossing your brothers into the street? By finding ways to destroy your sisters? Will that satisfy you?" she demanded.

"Yes!" The word escaped in a harsh whisper, ripped from the deepest part of him. "Yes, that would satisfy me."

"Because you'd win. Because then everyone would know that Reginald should have acknowledged you from the start because you're the best of all his sons, of all his daughters. Better than Matthew. Better than RJ. Better than Laurel and Kara and Lily. And once you've proven that, then what, Jack? What will you be left with?"

"The Kincaid Group."

"A shell. A shell without a heart and soul because you'd have carved the heart and soul out of it. A business is just a thing. Oh, don't you get that?" A heartbreaking urgency filled her voice. "It's the people who run it, who create it, who shape it…that's what makes it great."

"You're saying I can't provide the heart and soul?"

Didn't he see? "I'm saying that if you cut your family out of the business, you'll also cut part of yourself out, as well. You may not realize it at first because you'll be too busy celebrating what you perceive as a win. But eventually you'll discover how cold and sterile the business has become. How lonely and passionless. That it *is* just a business. That you've destroyed something that can't be replaced."

"The heart and soul?" he asked dryly.

She nodded. "At some point you'll realize what you've managed to win doesn't give you any satisfaction."

"I can live with that."

She stepped back. "But I can't."

He followed the path of her retreat. "What will it take to convince you to sign your proxy over to me?"

His question brought home how vast the chasm separating them was and made her want to cry. Instead, she lifted chin and faced him down. "Nothing. Nothing you can say will convince me to do that."

"So, you're going to give RJ your proxy?"

"It's what Reginald wanted, what he once told me he intended. I owe it to your father to respect his wishes."

She saw it then. The deep, unfathomable pain of having his father—once again—put his legitimate son ahead of his bastard. "Jack, it doesn't have to be like this."

"I think it does."

Desperation drove her to try anything she could to resolve the conflict between them. "I still have a wish from the bachelor auction. You owe it to me."

He simply shook his head. "That's not going to work, Nikki."

But maybe it would. Maybe there was one final person who could sway Jack, who could convince him to change his course and choose a new path, one that led to new beginnings instead of revenge. It was a risk. A hideous risk. And one that forced her to break her word to Reginald. Would he have understood? Would he have supported her decision? She closed her eyes, praying she was making the right choice. Because if she was wrong… As though in response to her prayer, a morning dove landed on the railing and cooed a soft benediction, one that felt like approval.

Taking a deep breath, Nikki opened her eyes. "I'll give you my proxy under one condition," she informed him.

That gave him pause. "Name it."

"You read your father's letter. You read your father's letter—and I mean out loud at the board meeting—and I'll give you my proxy." She could see the refusal building in his gaze, see him pulling back and shutting down.

"I'll read it, but not at the board meeting. Not out loud."

"It's my wish, Jack. You gave me a wish and I'm calling it due." She pushed and pushed hard. "Unless you're a man who doesn't honor his promises?"

He swore, long and virulently. "I can't believe you'd demand that of me. Whatever is in that letter is private and not something I intend to share with the Legitimates."

"I'm sorry, Jack." And she was. But she couldn't think of any other way to heal the breach between him and his Kincaid family. She could only trust that whatever Reginald wrote would help complete the reconciliation that had begun with Elizabeth and steadily worked its way through the rest of the family until only RJ remained. "Do you agree?"

He clamped his back teeth together. "I agree."

But everything about him, from his tense posture, to the blatant frustration and fury glittering in his eyes, to the growl that underscored his words, warned that he resented being forced to concede. No doubt she'd pay for that. Of course, she'd already figured that out, already allowed the hope of "happily ever after" to fade like the distant memory of an impossibly sweet dream.

He took a single step in her direction. "Shall we seal the deal like we did at the bachelor auction?"

He didn't give her time to react. He fisted his hands in the collar of her robe and pulled her up to meet his kiss, a hard, ruthless demand. It tasted of anger, laced with passion. It spoke of pain, underscored by hunger. It felt like a man pushed to the brink, lashing out. And yet, she sensed a hint of the tenderness that always flavored their lovemaking. She gave everything within her without hesitation, meeting his demand with her own. Showing her love in the only way she had left, knowing he'd reject the words, but couldn't quite turn from the desire that connected them. Bound them and made them one.

He tugged at the sash of her robe, loosening it. The silk parted, opening to him, just as she had always opened to him. He swept his hands over her. Memorizing her... Branding her... Saying goodbye. Tears filled her eyes and she wrapped her arms around him and savored these final moments together. When he released her and stepped back, she knew it was over. Could feel the deliberate withdrawal, the icing over of emotion and intent.

"I suggest we discuss where we go from here," he informed her.

He turned his back on her and crossed to the railing. He planted his hands on the salt-treated wood and stared out at the ocean. It was calm today, an ironic dichotomy to his turbulent relationship with Nikki. Although he'd suggested they discuss their next step, he had no idea what it might be.

He'd trusted her. Opened himself to her in ways he never had with any other woman. He'd let her in and she'd betrayed him. He didn't know how to deal with it. Did he end the affair? Consider himself fortunate that she hadn't really accepted the engagement ring he'd offered? Everything within him rejected the mere thought. He didn't want to end things between them.

Okay, fine. So they'd renegotiate their agreement. They'd start over and this time he'd set very clear parameters. First, all cards on the table. No lies. No secrets. And they'd go slow. Maybe that had been part of the initial problem. From the moment they met, from the moment they'd first touched, passion had exploded between them. Neither of them had been able to think straight, mainly because they couldn't keep their hands off each other. So, this time around he'd put rational thought ahead of sexual need. They would approach their relationship with calm, cool deliberation. He'd treat it the exact same way he did business, with logical steps that led to an ultimate end goal.

"Here's what I've decided," he announced. He gripped the railing and hoped like hell he could convince her to go along with the plan. "We'll continue seeing each other. But there will be ground rules. If you can't agree to them, better we call it off now."

He waited for her to protest, to tell him in no uncertain terms where to get off. It had always been one of the characteristics he most appreciated about Nikki.

They just needed to open negotiations so he'd know they still had a chance. She didn't respond and he turned, her name on his lips…only to discover her gone.

Ten

The next five days were the longest Nikki could remember.

One by one they crept by while the day of the board meeting marched ever closer. Everything seemed to hang by a frayed thread over a bottomless precipice. Alan continued to elude the police. Jack didn't call. And Nikki constantly worried about the bargain she'd made with him—whether it had been a smart decision or the stupidest of her life. She also worried about whether Reginald's letter would help, or make matters worse—assuming they could get any worse than they already were.

And all the while she grieved Jack's absence. Better get used to it, she warned herself, since that wasn't likely to change, even after the board meeting. Not only did Jack despise her, but once she signed over her proxy, the Kincaids would despise her, too.

She closed her eyes, fighting tears. Without Jack, her bed had become a cold and lonely place. Guilt kept her up most nights, adding to her exhaustion. Worst of all, she missed him with an intensity that physically hurt. Missed talking to him. Missed their laughter. Missed curling up on the couch with him while they read or watched TV. Missed how those quiet times so often turned to an equally quiet passion where books dropped to the floor or the TV was turned off and they slipped into each other's arms…and into each other.

There were so many little things she'd taken for granted. Like the way he'd pull her into his arms and spoon her tight against him during the night. How she'd wake to his kiss, to his lovemaking. The casual breakfasts they enjoyed on the deck or at the kitchen table, while they shared a cup of coffee and revealed their innermost thoughts and feelings. She longed for a return of those quick phone calls during the day that were a more effective jolt than any amount of caffeine. Not to mention the end of her workday and that sweet, breathless moment when she first saw him again. The anticipation of the coming embrace, after which they'd talk and nuzzle, mating scent and touch and bodies. Nikki closed her eyes and gave in to tears that came with increasing regularity—no doubt in part hormonal.

She'd lost Jack and had no idea how she'd ever fill the emptiness that loss created.

He'd lost Nikki and had no idea how he'd ever fill the emptiness that loss created.

Somehow she'd become an integral part of his life, filling up all the holes with her laughter and generosity. With her boundless love. Right from the start, she'd accepted him when no one else would, proving it by bidding an outrageous sum for a simple dinner. Well, and a wish, one he would give a substantial portion of his bank balance to take back.

That didn't change the fact that she possessed a unique capacity for forcing him to see what he'd rather avoid, to look at his life from a fresh perspective. More often than not he didn't care for the view, perhaps because it caused him to alter a course he'd set in stone a very long time ago. Too long ago.

It wasn't simply the passion they shared, though that went far beyond anything he'd ever believed possible. No, what drew him to her was something far more basic. He'd fallen in love with who she was at the core. Not only did she treat him with innate kindness and acceptance, she treated everyone that way, without artifice or pretense, but with a genuine spontaneity intrinsic to her character.

He crossed to his dresser and removed the sapphire and diamond engagement ring Nikki had left there, along with his father's letter that he'd resisted opening for the past five plus months, perhaps because he instinctively knew the contents contained a terrible emotional burden. A dark coffee ring stained the creamy-white envelope from when he'd anchored the letter to his deck railing with his coffee cup. At the time, he'd considered the mark appropriate, a dark smudge that reflected his birthright...or birth wrong. A ring that connected all the Kincaids within its unfortunate darkness.

He tossed the envelope onto his bed and frowned. Somehow that darkness had faded over the past few weeks, easing and lightening the more he'd gotten to know his Kincaid family. He suspected Nikki bore responsibility for that, as well, the way she'd affected so many areas of his life. She'd pushed and prodded him out of the darkness and into the strong, unwavering light, relentless in forcing him to see the truth. Her truth. His frown deepened. Or was it hers?

All these years he'd stood on the outside, his vision obscured by the tightly shut doors and thick, plated windows he believed separated him from his father and the Legitimates. Perhaps those windows and doors had screwed with his perception. Maybe by opening them—as Nikki had done—he could finally see clearly. Or maybe Nikki had been right when she'd said that he wasn't the one on the outside, that he'd barricaded himself within his home, refusing to lower his defenses so others could join him. Was it possible?

He scrubbed his face, the shadow of a beard rasping against his hands. Hell. He could feel the grain of truth running through her observation, despite his resistance to the idea. Well, he'd promised to read his father's letter at the board meeting in the morning and he'd honor his promise. But he hadn't said he wouldn't read the damn thing beforehand. Decision made, he snatched up the letter and broke the seal.

And what he read ripped apart his tidy little world.

He was late.

Nikki sat at the conference room table and nervously checked her watch. The Kincaids had already gathered. Laurel sat next to Matt and occasionally murmured a comment in his ear. Lily and Kara were quietly chatting, while RJ stared at Nikki. She could feel his building suspicion regarding her presence there. A single folder sat squarely positioned in front of her, the only contents her proxy which she'd already signed over to Jack. Just as RJ opened his mouth to speak, Jack entered.

He appeared every inch the executive businessman in a suit and dress shirt in unrelenting black, along with a gray, black and maroon striped tie. Discreet bits of gold flashed at his wrists from both his Rolex and a pair of knotted cuff links. RJ rose and Jack waved him back into his seat then held out a preemptory hand to Nikki. Her throat went instantly dry. Praying her fingers wouldn't tremble, she passed him her folder.

He continued to stand, taking instant charge of the meeting. "This proxy gives me the fifty-five percent controlling interest in The Kincaid Group necessary to take over as President and CEO. We can go through the motions of a vote, but it wouldn't change the fact that I'm now in charge."

"What the hell…!" RJ shot to his feet again. "Who owns those ten percent shares? How did you get the proxy?"

Nikki steeled herself to meet RJ's furious gaze. "I own them. I inherited them from my grandfather, Todd Beaulyn, who was given them by Reginald when he expanded into the real estate market. I signed over my proxy to Jack this morning."

Voices exploded around the table, the Kincaids all talking at once. Jack waited them out. "Object all you want. It's a done deal. Next order of business…" He removed a sheaf of papers from his breast coat pocket, his gaze drifting to meet Nikki's. "This is the letter my— *our*—father left me, which I will read."

"What the hell do we care what Dad had to say to you?" RJ demanded.

"Maybe it's important." Matt caught his brother's arm and drew him back into his chair. "Besides, I want to hear what Dad wrote."

Swearing beneath his breath, RJ subsided and gave a reluctant jerk of his head to indicate his consent.

Jack smoothed out the pages and began to read, "'Dear Jack, in some ways this is the most difficult letter of all those I've written today. Although I owe each of you an apology for the selfish decisions I made during my lifetime, you were the one most injured by those choices.'"

He broke off, his gaze arrowing in on his brothers and sisters. "Just so you know, that's not true. Elizabeth was the one most injured. When I was conceived your parents hadn't met. I was an accident of birth. But afterward, when he found us again…" Jack shook his head. "He should have divorced your mother before he ever started an affair with mine."

Nikki watched the Kincaid siblings exchange quick, surprised glances. Laurel nodded in agreement. "Thanks, Jack. I didn't expect you to feel that way. As it happens, we agree with you on that point."

He inclined his head. "To continue… 'You lived your life in the shadows, never acknowledged, never enjoying the benefits that your brothers and sisters received their entire lives. I know how you longed for that legitimacy. To be part of the family we shared. To have a father attend all your sporting events and celebrate your school accolades. To be there in the evenings after work. To simply be available for something as basic as a game of catch. I wasn't even there for most of your birthdays. Nor was I there the day you needed me most, the day you almost died.'"

From across the room, Nikki caught the hitch in Kara's breath, knew how much the words affected her. Dampness gathered in her soft green eyes, along with sympathy. "Oh, Jack. Matt told us about that. I'm so sorry."

Nikki could tell Kara's sympathy caught him by surprise. He hesitated, as though not quite certain how to respond. Even Matt and RJ exchanged looks that clearly acknowledged that Jack had received the short end of the "father" stick.

"It's okay. I survived," Jack finally said. He fumbled with the pages, looking for his place before continuing. "He goes on to say, 'I wasn't there for you, Jack, not the way I was for the others. And for that I apologize. I apologize for my weakness in trying to have the best of both worlds—the society my family held in too high esteem and the two women I loved too well…and not well enough. I have always loved you and been proud of the son I never claimed. And I apologize for my weakness in attempting to take too much from life without giving enough in return. I ask your forgiveness—'"

His voice faltered, broke off, and in that instant, Nikki realized he couldn't go on. She shot to her feet. This was her fault. Entirely her fault. She'd put him in this position without considering how intensely personal Reginald's letter might be, or how difficult he'd find it to read to his brothers and sisters. She'd merely hoped that his father had explained his decision in never acknowledging Jack and thereby help to heal the breach between the two families. She crossed to his side and slipped the creased pages from his hands.

"Don't," she murmured. "I'm sorry. I should never have asked you to read it aloud." She turned her attention to the Kincaids. "This is all my fault. I agreed to sign over my proxy if Jack promised to read his letter here today. I should never have put him through that."

"No." Jack's jaw set. "I going to finish it. I want to finish it."

"We get the idea," Matt said gently. "It's not necessary to read more. We understand why you have it in for us and for The Kincaid Group. I suspect I'd feel the same in your place." His sisters nodded in agreement while RJ stared at the table, his jaw set in a mirror image of Jack's.

"I said I'd finish it and I will." He took the letter from Nikki and snapped it open. Clearing his throat, he continued, though a desperate roughness filtered through his voice. "'I ask your forgiveness, not only for myself, but for your brothers and sisters. You should have been a brother to them from the beginning. I suspect you would have benefitted from that contact, just as their lives would have been far richer having you part of theirs. Believe it or not, you and RJ are very much alike, both with many of the same strengths… and weaknesses. I hope you won't allow the weaknesses you share to prevent you from having the relationship I denied you all these years. I'm opening a door, son, a door that I kept closed.'"

Jack paused. He looked up then and quoted the rest of the words from memory. "'I've left you forty-five percent interest in The Kincaid Group to help make up for all I neglected to give you, all I neglected to be for you. But I've also given you the shares so you would have a choice. To walk through the door I've now opened and be the man I know in my heart you are. Or you can close and lock that door…and have your vengeance. It's your choice, Jack.'"

He folded the letter and returned it to his coat pocket. Silence gripped the room, a silence so profound Nikki swore she could hear every breath taken, the beat of each heart. Slowly, RJ stood and looked at Jack. For the first time regret instead of antagonism colored his expression. "I wish Dad had raised us together. And I for one am sorry for what he did, how you were made to feel an outsider. I think for the first time I understand why you would choose vengeance and I really can't blame you. I wish you'd make a different choice, but I probably would make the same one if I were standing in your shoes."

Matt climbed to his feet, as did the women. One by one, they came to him. Embraced him. RJ was the last to approach. He held out his hand and waited. Jack didn't hesitate. He took it in a firm shake.

"If you'll all sit down again, we'll finish this," Jack said. "Before we continue, there is one personal detail I'd like to resolve." He turned to Nikki and took her hand in his. "A week ago you agreed to marry me. I'd like to know if you intend to honor our engagement."

For a split second Nikki couldn't move, couldn't think. Didn't dare hope. His steady gaze remained on her, open and unguarded. Intuition warned that she could shatter him with the least wrong word. "You still want to marry me?" she asked cautiously.

"Yes. The question is…do *you* want to marry *me?* You know who I am. What I am. What I intend to do. Do you stand with me or against me?"

"Oh, Jack." Tears overflowed her eyes and she

swiped at them with a trembling hand. "Don't you know by now? I've always stood with you."

For a long moment Jack couldn't move, couldn't think, the rush of relief was so profound. He closed his eyes for a brief moment and a muscle clenched in his jaw before easing. Thank God. He didn't know what he'd have done if she'd rejected him. He retrieved the engagement ring from his pocket, the sapphire a perfect match for her eyes, the diamonds a perfect match for her tears, and slipped it onto her finger. Then he gathered her close and kissed her. "I love you," he whispered against her mouth. "Trust me. That's all I've ever wanted—for you to love and trust me."

"I do trust you." Passion gleamed in her eyes, along with unmistakable faith. "And I love you with all my heart."

"Then let's get this over with." She returned to her seat and Jack's gaze swept his brothers and sisters, all of whom eyed him with an understandable wariness. This next part would be almost as difficult as reading his father's letter and he suspected it would end any possibility of a relationship with the Kincaids. "At this point you should know that a few hours ago the police arrested my brother, Alan Sinclair, for the murder of our father."

His words fell like a bombshell.

"Nikki and I had begun to suspect him a few weeks ago and have been working hard to gather the evidence to prove his guilt. Alan has confessed, claiming he killed Dad in order to prevent him from cutting off future financial assistance. Apparently, Alan believed our mother would inherit a generous amount, enough to keep him in the lap of luxury for the rest of his pathetic life. I had no idea or I'd have done everything within my power to stop him. I know nothing I can say will make up for what he's done. But I'm more sorry than I can express that I'm in any way related to that sorry son of a bitch."

Matt shot Jack a grim look. "I second that motion and vote in favor of his rotting in prison for the rest of his miserable life."

"Seconded," Laurel said.

"I believe that's one motion we can all agree on," Lily stated, her eyes flashing with anger. She turned a hint of her anger on Jack. "But if you think we blame you for his actions, you're crazy."

"Once again, I second the motion," Matt said.

He elbowed RJ, who nodded in reluctant agreement. "I hold you accountable for plenty, Sinclair, but not that."

Jack gave a brisk nod. "I appreciate it. If you have any other questions about the situation, Detective Mc-Donough is available to fill you in. At this point, I intend to move onto new business."

"Give it to us straight," RJ insisted. "We're now Carolina Shipping and anyone with the last name Kincaid is out of a job, right?"

Jack smiled. "Not quite. My next motion is to bring Carolina Shipping under The Kincaid Group umbrella."

"Wait." Laurel leaned forward, frowning. "You're going to fold your company into ours? Not the other way around?"

"Not the other way around," Jack confirmed. He crossed to the conference room door and opened it. "Harold, if you'd come in now."

Harold Parsons, the Kincaid lawyer entered the

room, clutching a packet of papers. He nodded to the group at large. "I'd like to state for the record that I don't appreciate being dragged out of bed at the crack of dawn to take care of matters which should have—and could have—been addressed weeks ago."

"Understood," Jack replied. "I'm sure your appreciation, or lack thereof, will be reflected in my bill."

"Count on it," the lawyer snapped.

"What's going on?" RJ demanded.

"Harold is about to pass out documents that reapportion the shares of TKG."

RJ shot to his feet. "You can't do that."

"Yes, I can. And yes, I have." Jack lifted an eyebrow. "Unless you don't want a fifteen percent share in the business to replace the nine percent you currently own?"

RJ started to reply, then broke off with a look of utter confusion. "Come again?"

"As I started to say, I'm reapportioning the shares of TKG so each of us owns an equal amount, which comes to fifteen percent apiece. Nikki, of course, will continue to control the ten percent share left to her by her grandfather. Once you sign, we'll vote on my next motion which is for RJ to take over as CEO and President, while I head up the shipping end of the organization, which includes Carolina Shipping. I will remain in full control of this particular TKG asset. I assume Matt will continue as Director of New Business. And I'm hoping that Nikki will stay on as our corporate investigator." He paused. "Any objections? No, I didn't think so. In that case, the motion passes. Next order of business…"

Before any of his brothers or sisters had time to recover from their shock, he swung his bride-to-be into his arms. "Nikki and I are leaving for the rest of the day. Don't bother calling. Neither of us will be answering our cell phones." And with that, he left the room.

Behind him, voices exploded in excitement. He simply smiled. *Okay, Dad, I opened the door. Let's see who decides to walk through.*

As it turned out, the entire Kincaid family walked through the door Jack opened. At Elizabeth's insistence, they broke with tradition and every last one of them showed up on his doorstep midday Sunday, loaded down with an endless stream of hot dishes. Fragrant scents wafted from the various containers. And every last one of his guests greeted him with a hug and kiss, or a manly handshake and a slap on the back. He didn't know quite what to make of it all.

They all oohed and aahed over the house…and then made themselves right at home, filling it to overflowing with family.

Nikki spotted Jack's confusion and laughed. "Just go with it," she advised. "You opened the door and here they all are."

"Well, hell. I was thinking one at a time, not everyone at once."

"Deal with it." She wrapped her arms around his waist. "All or nothing is often how it works with family, Jack. It's one of the fun parts."

"I'll take your word for it." He snatched a quick kiss then sank in for another deeper one. "I'm hungry."

"Good thing there's lots of food."

Jack shook his head. "I'm not hungry for food."

She grinned, wagging her finger at him. "That's all

you're getting until we're alone again. Come on." She caught his hand in hers and tugged him toward the dining room. "Let's go join your family."

Angela showed up in the middle of the mass confusion surrounding the organization of dinner. Startled to find the Kincaids there, she started to make her excuses. Elizabeth stopped her, drawing her off to one side. Jack stiffened, seeing the unmistakable lines of tension that invaded the two women. This had all the makings of two trains on the same track, headed for a collision. He hesitated, not certain whether he should let them talk through their differences or if he should intercede. He wasn't the only one watching with bated breath. So were Elizabeth's daughters.

"Trust my mom," RJ advised, coming up behind Jack and clapping him on the shoulder. "She knows Angela is in a bad place and that in order to have you as part of our family, it means finding a way to work out her differences with your mother. I promise, she won't make the situation any worse. And maybe, just maybe, getting to know each other will help them come to terms with old history, not to mention their grief over Dad's death."

Even as Jack watched, he saw the two women shed tears, then embrace. "Your mother is an unusual lady," he said slowly. "Not many women would show such kindness and generosity toward their husband's mistress."

"She's one of a kind." Pride filled RJ's voice.

Once Angela had been welcomed into the fold, the organization of the meal was like watching a coordinated assault. Plates and silver appeared on his dining room table, followed by food and drinks. Someone found his stereo system and turned on background music. Then they all took their seats, somehow forming a pattern of brothers and sisters, in-laws and parents, until they'd jumbled together in a companionable mix.

Jack had expected some awkwardness over their first meal together. Instead, he found it—well, maybe not one-hundred-percent comfortable—but certainly lighthearted and fun. "Comfortable" would occur over time, he suspected. The thought brought with it a rush of unexpected pleasure. He had that time now, had the opportunity to build a relationship with these people, to create what he'd never truly had…a family.

He also learned a lot about the Kincaids that he'd never known before. He discovered that the baby Lily and Daniel were expecting any day now was a son, and since they'd married quietly at the courthouse so they wouldn't steal Kara's thunder by having a wedding right before hers, the soon-to-be parents intended to renew their vows in a huge celebration in October. He also learned that Kara's husband, Eli, had first been engaged to Laurel. Of course, Jack could tell just by looking at Eli and Laurel that they didn't share any sort of chemistry. Fortunately, nature had taken its course and the appropriate sister had discovered her perfect partner. Laurel glowed with unmistakable love and her husband, Rakin, announced that the Kincaids could expect an influx of new business thanks to his Middle Eastern business connections.

Most intriguing of all was when RJ and Brooke admitted they were also expecting a baby, the mother-to-be blushing prettily. The instant the news came out, Elizabeth returned her fork to her plate and eyed her children one by one. "Clearly, I didn't explain how this is supposed to work," she informed them in true matriarch fashion. "So, listen up. First we marry *then* we get pregnant. Are we clear on the order from this point forward?"

Lily and Brooke exchanged quick grins. "Yes, Mom," they said in unison.

"Just practicing," Brooke added, "for when we're married and I get to call you Mom for real."

Tears welled up in Elizabeth's eyes and she cleared her throat before speaking. "No need for you to wait. It's lovely having another daughter to call me Mom, as well as having another grandchild on the way." Elizabeth picked up her fork again. "I will add there are the occasional exceptions to premarital pregnancies which serve to prove the rule." She glanced at Jack and smiled with sincere warmth. "And for which I, personally, am very grateful."

"I propose a toast," RJ said, holding up his glass. "Here's to all of us."

"To new beginnings," Lily called out.

"To creating a home," Nikki added.

Matt shot Jack a shrewd look. "To unlocking doors and opening windows."

Jack was the last to lift his glass. He could feel the final protective barriers give way and reached for Nikki's hand, gripping it hard. It felt good to be free of those barriers, better than he could have believed possible. He allowed the last of his resistance to be swept away, allowed himself to embrace and accept what he'd secretly longed for ever since he was a teenager who'd been told he'd never be accepted by his father.

His gaze swept the table before settling on Nikki. "Most of all…here's to family," he said.

* * *

Much later that evening, Jack and Nikki wandered onto the deck, and wrapped each other in a warm embrace. "It all turned out well, didn't it?" he asked.

She leaned her head against his shoulder and released a sigh of blatant satisfaction. "It did, yes."

He kissed her, a slow, lingering kiss. "Thank you, Nikki."

"For what?"

"For giving me a family."

She smiled, a secretive little curve of lips that tempted him to kiss her again. "A family that's about to grow larger."

He chuckled at the memory of Elizabeth's motherly reprimand. "Thanks to Lily and Daniel, and Brooke and RJ. And despite Elizabeth's disapproval."

"Mmm. I'm afraid she has even more reason to disapprove."

He stilled. "What do you mean?"

"Exactly what you suspect I mean." She snuggled in close. "I think you'll make a wonderful father. Don't you?"

He struggled to reply, the words catching in his throat. "I'm going to be a father?"

A hint of concern slid into Nikki's sapphire gaze. "Will that be a problem for you?"

"No," he said slowly. "In fact, I think I'm going to be a great father."

Nikki smiled in satisfaction. "So do I."

Jack gazed out over the ocean waves toward the horizon, realizing he'd finally achieved everything he'd ever wanted. By letting down his defenses, he'd won his heart's desire—a home and family, filled with the

sort of love and happiness he and Nikki would bring to
it. And a child. Their child. A product of enduring love
and the first step toward their future together.

If he listened carefully enough, he could practically
hear that future. Could hear his home ring with youthful
footsteps, the sound of their voices echoing off walls
that would eventually know generations of love and
laughter. To be a father to them, there day after day,
participating in each and every phase of their lives. To
grow old with the woman he loved, with the relatives
he'd so recently claimed and the children they were
busily creating. Oh, he could hear that future, all right.

Hear it filling his home to overflowing.

Hear it filling his life with love.

Hear it gifting him with the most precious of all
commodities…

A family.

* * * * *

REQUEST YOUR FREE BOOKS!

2 FREE NOVELS PLUS 2 FREE GIFTS!

ALWAYS POWERFUL, PASSIONATE AND PROVOCATIVE

YES! Please send me 2 FREE Harlequin Desire® novels and my 2 FREE gifts (gifts are worth about $10). After receiving them, if I don't wish to receive any more books, I can return the shipping statement marked "cancel." If I don't cancel, I will receive 6 brand-new novels every month and be billed just $4.30 per book in the U.S. or $4.99 per book in Canada. That's a saving of at least 14% off the cover price! It's quite a bargain! Shipping and handling is just 50¢ per book in the U.S. and 75¢ per book in Canada.* I understand that accepting the 2 free books and gifts places me under no obligation to buy anything. I can always return a shipment and cancel at any time. Even if I never buy another book, the two free books and gifts are mine to keep forever.

225/326 HDN FEF3

Name	(PLEASE PRINT)

Address	Apt. #

City	State/Prov.	Zip/Postal Code

Signature (if under 18, a parent or guardian must sign)

Mail to the **Reader Service:**

IN U.S.A.: P.O. Box 1867, Buffalo, NY 14240-1867
IN CANADA: P.O. Box 609, Fort Erie, Ontario L2A 5X3

Not valid for current subscribers to Harlequin Desire books.

Want to try two free books from another line?
Call 1-800-873-8635 or visit www.ReaderService.com.

* Terms and prices subject to change without notice. Prices do not include applicable taxes. Sales tax applicable in N.Y. Canadian residents will be charged applicable taxes. Offer not valid in Quebec. This offer is limited to one order per household. All orders subject to credit approval. Credit or debit balances in a customer's account(s) may be offset by any other outstanding balance owed by or to the customer. Please allow 4 to 6 weeks for delivery. Offer available while quantities last.

Your Privacy—The Reader Service is committed to protecting your privacy. Our Privacy Policy is available online at www.ReaderService.com or upon request from the Reader Service.

We make a portion of our mailing list available to reputable third parties that offer products we believe may interest you. If you prefer that we not exchange your name with third parties, or if you wish to clarify or modify your communication preferences, please visit us at www.ReaderService.com/consumerschoice or write to us at Reader Service Preference Service, P.O. Box 9062, Buffalo, NY 14269. Include your complete name and address.

Harlequin *Blaze*™

red-hot reads

Three men dare to live up to naughty reputations....

Leslie Kelly

Janelle Denison and Julie Leto

bring you a collection of steamy stories in

THE GUY MOST LIKELY TO...

Underneath It All

When Seth Crowder goes back for his ten-year high school reunion, he's hoping he'll finally get a chance with the one girl he ever loved. Lauren DeSantos has convinced herself she is over him...but Seth isn't going to let her walk away again.

Can't Get You Out of My Head

In high school, cheerleader Ali Seaver had the hots for computer nerd Will Beckman but stayed away in fear of her reputation. Now, ten years later, she's ready to take a chance and go for what she's always wanted.

A Moment Like This

For successful party planner Erica Holt, organizing her high school reunion provides no challenge—until sexy Scott Ripley checks "yes" on his RSVP, revving Erica's sex drive to its peak.

Available July wherever books are sold.

New York Times *and* USA TODAY *bestselling author Vicki Lewis Thompson returns with yet another irresistible cowpoke! Meet Mathew Tredway—cowboy, horse whisperer and honorary Son of Chance.*

Read on for a sneak peek from the bestselling miniseries SONS OF CHANCE:

LEAD ME HOME Available July 2012 only from Harlequin® Blaze™.

As Matthew returned to the corral and Houdini, the taste of Aurelia's mouth was on his lips and her scent clung to his clothes. He'd briefly satisfied the craving growing within him, and like a light snack before a meal, it would have to do.

When he'd first walked into the kitchen, his mind had been occupied with the challenge of training Houdini. He'd thought his concentration would hold long enough to get some carrots, ask about the corn bread and leave before succumbing to Aurelia's appeal. He'd miscalculated. Within a very short time, desire had claimed every brain cell.

Although seducing her this morning was out of the question, his libido had demanded some sort of satisfaction. He'd tried to deny that urge and had nearly made it out of the house. Apparently his willpower was no match for the temptation of Aurelia's mouth, though, and he'd turned around.

If he'd ever felt this kind of desperate need for a woman, he couldn't recall it. During the night, as he'd lain in his narrow bunk listening to the cowhands snore, he'd searched for an explanation as to why Aurelia affected him this way.

Sometime in the early-morning hours he'd come up with

the answer. After years of dating women who were rolling stones like he was, he'd developed an itch for a hearth-and-home kind of woman. Aurelia, with her cooking skills and voluptuous body, could give him that.

With luck, once he'd scratched this particular itch, he'd be fine again. He certainly hoped so, because he had no intention of giving up his career, and travel was a built-in requirement. Plus he liked to travel and had no real desire to stay in one spot and become domesticated.

Tonight he'd say all that to Aurelia, because he didn't want her going into this with any illusions about permanence. He figured that when the right guy came along, she'd get married and have kids.

Too bad that guy wouldn't be him....

Will Aurelia be the one to corral this cowboy for good?
Find out in: LEAD ME HOME

Available July 2012
wherever Harlequin® Blaze™ books are sold.

This summer, celebrate everything Western
with Harlequin® Books!
www.Harlequin.com/Western

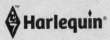
Harlequin®

nocturne™

Take a bite out of summer!

Enjoy three tantalizing tales from
Harlequin® Nocturne™ fan-favorite authors

MICHELE HAUF,
Kendra Leigh Castle
and Lisa Childs

VACATION
WITH A VAMPIRE

Available July 2012!
Wherever books are sold.